I0615948

Saved by Grace...

"Walking through life's afflictions into God's deliverance..."

Dr. AUDREYANN C. MOSES

2nd Edition

AUDREYANN C. MOSES

DEDICATION

This book is dedicated to normal everyday Christian families who love each other despite family dysfunction. Remember, although we try hard to live a certain way and raise our children a certain way, nobody's perfect and Jesus loves us with open arms... anyway...

"Your grace and mercy brought me through."

Acknowledgements

*I would like to thank all of the wonderful people that God put in my life, specifically to help me write. I'd like to thank my friend and coach, Denise Mock, who helped turn a few words, written in 1997 on a restaurant napkin, into **Saved By Grace**... Thank you Valerie Baty who painstakingly read a draft full of my voice with many errors and turned it into my voice in English. Thank you to Lyndia Belcher, Ronny Mock, Annie Gilchrist and Pamela Anderson who read drafts and gave me their brutal, but loving opinion. Thank you to my husband, Leonard, who helped brainstorm, "the rest of the story." Thank you to my sons, LJ and Stefan Moses, for helping me get the "facts" straight.*

*And, thank YOU for trusting that "**Saved by Grace**..." is worth the time to read.*

Enjoy!

CONTENTS

SAVED BY GRACE

CHAPTER ONE

The Restaurant

Shortly after I moved to Beaufort, South Carolina, I decided to go to this quaint little restaurant that I heard about for lunch. It sits on a side street corner in downtown Beaufort, as if it owned the entire block. As you walk inside, it's southern... it's charming... it's Gullah. My friend use to say that the only thing that makes food Gullah is the spices and okra, otherwise you were eating regular soul food. The restaurant had this southern mixed with African décor that mesmerized you. And, if you let it, it very well would take you to another place and time. It quickly became one of my favorite restaurants.

For quite some time I was the only black patron in the restaurant, which was very interesting considering the type of food served. I don't remember noticing that, before. I'm not sure why I noticed it, today. There were sailors, business people, and college students, but it did puzzle me as to why I was the "only one."

Now, on the one hand, it could be because it is still early in the lunch hour, around 11:00am. I came early and had plans to perch here for several hours to write. And, on the other hand, maybe there is a story as to why there were no black people patronizing this restaurant. Maybe, there had been some scandal involving the restaurant. Like, maybe the original owners of this corner were a black family whose family member was murdered and the restaurant was swindled out from under them by the grandparents of the current owner; or maybe, it was sold at auction due to foreclosure; or even, acquired as payment for a gambling debt and the new owner promised not to change the name. Then again, maybe the restaurant was being boycotted, in protest, for not hiring black chefs and management. Only if you weren't from this area, like me, you wouldn't know what really happened. No one seemed to be concerned or excited by me being there, so I decided maybe it was just too early or the wrong day of the week.

Then just as I was looking at the menu and happy that pork wasn't in everything, in walked two black women who did not have that "lovers-of-excitement-and-adventure" look about them, but they just were here to eat after a very boring church board meeting. Then the mailman, black, dawned in his raincoat and safari hat, which covered jheri curls, walked in. He politely walked through nodding to the customers, including me, delivered the mail and left. The music was excellent. Bowie, Bon Jovi, Roberta Flack, Phoebe Snow and the Elton John style music, is just what I needed.

Later, a business-looking couple walked in. They were prim and proper. He took her umbrella and held the chair for her. I was thinking you don't see that much anymore. They didn't speak to anyone and barely spoke to each other. Maybe they were making a very serious decision. Maybe they had just left a very important meeting to purchase property to build a chain of private owned shops. Or, maybe they are breaking up a relationship... an affair that is getting to serious and he's worried that his wife knows. He can't divorce her, because she owns 51% of his business. His cellular phone rings. It's his wife asking him where he is and of course he says he working through lunch. The reason she called is to let him know that she will be working late as well. Wonder if he knows that, while he is breaking up an affair, she has started one?

So, as it is my custom, I am sitting, enjoying my tea, and imagining the lives of the people that walk in and out. And, I am thinking, something here will make a great book.

I was so busy watching this one and that one trying to decide who they were and why, that I didn't notice the restaurant was packed. There were no seats – not even at the bar, which is understandable, because this restaurant is very popular. And, I was no longer the "only one."

I was sitting close to the entrance of the restaurant. A conversation taking place between the host and a woman with a desire to have lunch caught my attention. The host informed her that it would be a wait for a table. I had not yet placed my ordered. I told the host, if she didn't mind sitting with a stranger, I would share my table with her. She was very grateful. We started chatting. I introduced myself and I told her this was one of my favorite restaurants and she said she had only been here one other time a little more than a year ago. I told her that I come here often to write, because the atmosphere is so thought provoking… to say the least. She asked me about my previous books. I told her I'm sure she had not heard of me, unless she has read self-help books on personal growth, self-improvement or problems in dysfunctional, trying to be Christian families. I told her, "I'm starting a new book, but at this point, I'm not sure what to write about. I normally write a combination of fiction and non-fiction, because I'm a psychologist and have only written within my field… scientific, empirical studies and research etc.; however, I decided I wanted to just write about something intriguing and fun. So, I've been people-watching and making up stories about them to see where my imagination takes me."

She looked at me with this sorrowful glare and I felt as if I needed to apologize. I asked her, "Had I said something wrong?" She said, "How would you like to write a true story about a dysfunctional almost-Christian family from the south?" Now, I'm just looking at her. I asked her, "What do you mean, a true story?" She said, "My life, for the last few years, could only be believed if you read it in a paperback on a long flight." "You don't know anything about me," I said to her. "I might be a National Inquirer reporter, for all you know." She smiled and said, "I doubt that, you have good eyes and I don't think you will discredit me or this story." "Besides, once you hear it, you will be happy to write it." I smiled, and said, "I'm all ears and could I record while you talk." She said, "No problem."

And, so she talked. I listened and made notes.

CHAPTER TWO

Meeting #1:

"Guess Who I Saw Today?"

As our food arrived, Lizanne began her story…

"My name is Lizanne Martin and I almost lost the best second husband a woman could ever ask for. The last time I was here was a little over a year ago and that day my world started to crumble around me and you know what, it was my fault."

Lizanne laughed, as she said, "Well, I guess like any great story, I'll start in the middle."

Lizanne began to talk. "Do you know the song 'Guess Who I Saw Today' by Nancy Wilson?" I said I knew who Nancy Wilson was. *She recommended I listen to the song as soon as I got a chance.*

About a year ago, I was sitting at a table on the other side of the bar, enjoying an early evening cocktail with my sister-in-law, when I noticed a couple come into the restaurant and sit over there. *Lizanne gestured to a corner near the bar where, instead of tables, there were lounge chairs and small round tables where customers could meet, chat, have a drink and hors d'oeuvres. As she continued, I could see distress in her expression.*

At first, I wasn't sure what I was seeing and then the Nancy Wilson song started playing over the intercom. This restaurant has always played good jazz, but they could have picked any song but that one to play that day. My sister-in-law Maria turned around to see what I was looking at and the look on her face confirmed what I saw. It was my husband, her brother, and another woman we did not know. She started to jump up and run over there immediately; I stopped her."

"Maria was so distraught that she started speaking in Spanish and lucky for me I speak Spanish. I'm not going to tell you what she was saying."

"I told her not to move, because I know her. She would have gone over there and started screaming at him in Spanglish and hitting him or something, because that's what older sisters do – they are twins; however, she came first, so she lets him know that she is the oldest whenever it suits her."

"I wanted to think it was an innocent meeting. A new contractor… although, I would have known about that since I'm the company's contract manager, maybe an old friend, *anything* that doesn't resemble mistress. He had not mentioned anything about an upcoming lunch meeting. To be honest, I had not asked. And, to be even more honest, until that day, I didn't really care what he did. You see, I had neglected him for quite some time. After my first husband James died, I developed the ability to shut people out of my life when they started getting too close."

"So, I made Maria sit still to ensure he did not see us. It was a good thing we were about to leave when they walked in and that we were sitting in an area where he could not see us. I made her promise not to say anything to anyone, especially her husband, his best friend, until I figured out how to handle the situation. Maria was furious, but she agreed." *She kind of sat there for a moment, as if she was sorting out her emotions… as if she could feel everything now that she had felt that day -- should she care, be angry or just pretend she didn't*

6

see him.

"I tell you what, when I got home, I had no clue what I would do or say. My emotions were all over the place, because even though I was neglecting him, it didn't dawn on me that he would find someone else to show him affection. And ironically, when I turned on the radio, you will never guess what was playing... "Clean-Up Woman!!!" I just laid on the floor and cried for a minute. I did get myself together before he came in, because Maria called to find out if I was okay and what was I going to do; and I didn't want him to see me prostrate whimpering. I told her I decided not to say anything to him and although it was killing her, I made Maria promise again not to say anything to anyone. I needed to think."

"Well, as life would have it, the next day was work and the day after was work, and then it was the weekend and the next week and so on. I finally convinced Maria that the affair was nothing and I wasn't going to worry about it. I fell back into my "job more important" mode and although I didn't forget it, I didn't feel the need to ask him about it. I had other things to worry about, like how to keep our business afloat and be angry with him, because his brother put the business in jeopardy which is why I was in "neutral" with him... not in love and not out of love... just neutral, which is the worst place for a marriage. I even decided that if he is having an affair, good for him, because I wasn't interested... another bad place for a marriage to be."

"Honestly, if he was having an affair, it was my fault. Long before Antonio and I married I decided the only man that truly deserved my love was dead. I had taught myself to be selfish and closed minded, when it came to other men. I learned to contain my emotions so that when the next one, if there ever would be a next one, died, it wouldn't really matter. I know it was a terrible place for me to be in; I'm sure I needed therapy, probably still do, but that's where I was when Antonio came along. He and I knew each other many years ago (about 25ish years ago). We ran into each other again about five years ago. I should have just said no the first time he asked me out for dinner, but I was lonely after involuntarily being without my James. I said yes; I was weak that day. I don't have an excuse for saying yes to dancing, dining, inviting him to dinner and him inviting me to movies and courting and like I said, it was completely selfish. Maybe he may have been feeling selfish himself, at the time. I did warn Antonio and he said he could handle it. He was grieving a marriage broken and so in actuality, we were both on the rebound. Terrible state of affairs to start a relationship on, but nevertheless, that's where we started – pretty much already doomed."

She shook her head, as if to shake out the pain that these memories were gathering there. I asked her about herself, her childhood … she smiled and then frowned. She suggested we meet the next day. I agreed.

CHAPTER THREE

Meeting #2:

"The Websters"

Lizanne began telling me about herself and her family by saying,
"On September 9, 1974 I became an adult." Me, Lizanne
Maria Webster was on a plane for the first time in my life headed to
Naval Training Command Orlando Florida for Navy Boot Camp. I
had finally realized one of my lifelong dreams, all 18 years of it. It
was bittersweet for me, because my best friend was not here to
celebrate this transition of graduating from high school and joining
the United States Navy. For as long as I can remember, I've always
wanted to be in the Navy, be a sailor, well a WAVE (Women
Accepted for Volunteer Emergency Service) which is what women
in the navy were referred to in the '70s; but as far as I was concerned
there was nothing volunteer about my naval career goals and I was
a Sailor and would be one for the rest of my life. I actually enjoyed
boot camp; it was a breeze for me, because my dad was a preacher
and I could only get away with so much and after my mom died, I
lived in quite the dysfunctional household with my father and
brother, so nothing alarmed me. She gave a small smile and said "To
this date, my favorite military hymn is 'Waves of the Navy'."

Lizanne smiled when talking about her parents. "My parents
were almost perfect. I even loved my brother, Justin which was a
test in itself, because he was nerve-racking and always getting into

something. Not street trouble, just stupid boy trouble. He is six years younger than me so sometimes I felt like he was my child."

"He was full of energy from birth and was what most would identify as an ordinary young boy. We grew up in a small town about 100 miles from Charleston, SC. We were a Christian family and our Dad was the Pastor of our church. My dad's job transferred him to different churches every four years or so. We were at our current church for about one year."

"Justin was a pretty happy kid, got along with everyone. He especially loved church, which is unusual for a child his age; and so he developed a relationship with Christ early in his life. He loved the experiences he had in the church, especially the youth programs, the choir and Pathfinders (boy scouts) where he was on the drill team. His goal was to become captain of the drill team. He basically enjoyed his life."

"He didn't like that dad's job moved us from one church to another. It made it difficult to grow up with the friends he made, but he seem to adjust. His elementary school years were in a Christian school and when we moved he started in the Christian Academy near our church. He loved his school and was becoming interested in school extra curriculum activities. "

"I chose to attend the public high school, because they had an excellent foreign language program with the community college. My parents were not keen on allowing me to go to public school, however, despite the moving around I manage to maintain honor roll grades, well most of the time. I was an honor student in high school and actually graduated with honors. My grade point average afforded me an opportunity to go to one of the most prestigious colleges in South Carolina, but I wanted to join the Navy and be an interpreter."

"While trying to acclimate to his new school and schedule,

Justin began struggling in math. His teacher recommended a tutor for him, a "student with outstanding recommendations from the public high school to tutor him. His name was Wade Martin. He lived a few houses down from us which made it convenient for tutoring. Tutoring not only helped Justin in class, but he began to actually like math. I told my parents I knew Wade from school and I wasn't that keen on him. I saw the students he hung out with and it's amazing that he was an honor student. I heard he use to get in a lot of trouble, although he managed never to get arrested or sent to detention. It seemed that someone else always went in his place. He was more like an honor hoodlum."

"It turned out that Wade's story was kind of sad. Unfortunately for our family, Justin liked Wade. Justin talked about his activities at church during one of their tutoring sessions. He learned that even though Wade's mom went to church, he rarely went with her and she did not make him. Wade was not interested in church or anything dealing with church. Wade's biological parents divorced when he was five years old and his now ex-stepfather was a deacon in the church and abusive towards him and his mother at home. It was an oxy-moron – deacon and physical abuser. Somehow, those two activities were not supposed to mix, but in Wade's world it mixed like water and cement mix. Even though he and his father spent time together, Wade felt his father did not try hard enough to protect him and that God was not reliable. As far as Wade was concerned, he managed to survive his horrible life without his dad or God's help. It was hard for Justin to fathom not needing God, but soon he would experience those same doubts in God."

"When Justin was nine years old, our own lives begin to crumble around us. Our mother was diagnosed with cancer. We watched her get sicker and sicker. He and mom were very close and he just knew that God would heal her. He prayed every day for her to get better. After a year of surgery, chemo and radiation therapy, throwing up, hair and weight loss and anything else horrible you can imagine about cancer, she went into remission and was better for about a year, which gave Justin an opportunity to show Wade how good God is. Justin did not understand remission so he believed that God answered his prayers and for him our family life was back to normal. After about a year, my dad and I started to recognize signs that her remission might be reversing. A couple weeks after his eleventh birthday while he was still in school, our mom was rushed to the hospital. She was much sicker than before. Because he didn't understand remission, Justin was confused as to why God would allow her to become sick again. He wanted to believe that God would heal her again. But, she was getting worse as oppose to better."

"My mother tried to keep her spirits high and she continued to encourage us to maintain our faith in the Lord. She did not want mourning before or after her death. I watched as the cancer slowly dimmed the light in her eyes, however she was adamant that God's will is always right and that if we lived in accordance to that will we would all be together one day.

One night, I heard Justin bargaining with God to save her. I was in pain for him because it would be terrible if she died. And, she was dying."

"My dad felt guilty, because he had not paid enough attention to her in the beginning. He stayed at my mom's bedside caring for her as best he could. I could see both my mother and father wasting away. She was dying physically and he was dying emotionally and maybe even spiritually. As my mom worsened, Justin began to distance himself from her and God. The more reality was evident, the clearer it was that my family will never be the same again."

"She died, when Justin was twelve and I was seventeen and Justin was devastated that God would allow this to happen. No matter what anyone said, he blamed God and he became critical of anyone who didn't blame God, including dad and I. It didn't help that Wade fueled his distrust in God by reminding him that God is not trustworthy. Wade was no longer his tutor. but his ideology still influenced Justin in a negative way."

"So, the real reason I wanted to leave as soon as possible was because the death of my mom affected us in a negative way and our home was no longer home. My brother and father had evolved into people I could not deal with on a daily basis."
She stopped talking and took a very deep breath...
"I'm telling you before my mother died our family was perfect. My brother and I were blessed that our parents were in love with each other for real and raised us in a Christian home because some of my friends were really struggling. Their parents were not Christians and sometimes were not parents either. Two of my friends were pregnant and there was no support from their parents or the family of the father. Many of the kids at school didn't have a relationship with their fathers. My dad wasn't always home, but at least I knew who and where he was. I would invite my friends to all of the youth events at our church and sometimes my home would host a sleepover and they would play games and eat good food. It was fun times with my mother. My dad tried to be available for family events, but as the pastor of our church, he spent more time at the church and with the church members and did not notice my mother's declining health until it was too late."

"It was evident that my mom was the glue that held our family together. When she died, we fell apart. My father threw himself head and feet into the church, my brother left the family and the church, emotionally and I fled to the Navy as quickly as they were able to enlist me."

"Before I left for boot camp, I advised my dad to keep a hold on Justin and a watch on Wade because although he was grieving, Justin was a boy struggling to understand why God took his mother and his faith was in jeopardy. Wade was a bad influence and he needed to keep him away. Both my dad and brother were angry with me, because I decided to leave immediately after graduation and so they ignored my warnings about Wade and about Justin's faith in God. My dad realized the problem was a problem, when Justin was standing in front of a judge."

"So we buried our mother and within a few months, my family was invisible."

By now The Restaurant had become our official meeting place. Lizanne seemed a little weary today. She said she had a long night, her husband is ill. "I just needed a minute to myself, so I'm glad we had this meeting planned," she sighed. We found a table away from the crowd.

CHAPTER FOUR

Meeting #3: "Now What...?"

"When our mom died, Justin lost his way. He was still a boy and there was no one to help him find himself. Our father's grief over shadowed his responsibilities as a father. My grief sent me to the Navy, as soon as I graduated from high school – about four months after my mother's death. Even Wade was gone to live with his father. Justin's idea of life had changed 180 degrees. He dropped out of church. He went physically because dad didn't give him a choice, but he stopped emotionally participating in everything. He was just there. He began to be in and out of trouble at home, in the street and at school. Throughout his teenage years, he got into trouble, arrested and sent to juvenile detention. When he was arrested, his friends were not available to talk on his behalf, dad was angry and embarrassed, I was overseas, his mother was dead and God certainly didn't care about him."

"Nevertheless, much to everyone's amazement, Justin manage to come out of his stupor, recover his grades and graduate. Deep down he knew it was by the grace of God, but he was not going to admit it. He preferred to claim this victory as his determination not to be what the people in his life, especially church folk continually spoke on him – trifling', no-count, a heathen, mainly because he quit Pathfinders and the choir ... those sort of labels and worst. He determined in his spirit that he was not going to let these attacks and his setbacks keep him from making something of himself and leaving the misery of his life in South Carolina."

"He was accepted into college with a scholarship. Dad wanted to send him to a Christian college in Alabama, but Justin refused. He chose a college in South Carolina, away from home and moved on campus. He chose a career in accounting. Dad didn't understand why he chose accounting. There were accountants, tax offices and certified public accountants on every corner and he didn't see how he could be successful, especially with his criminal record. What dad did not know was that Justin actually enjoyed numbers and he had become good in math. Justin's plan was to graduate from college, with honors, leave South Carolina never to return, work for a big, prestigious firm and eventually start his own firm with big dollar clients. He will be so busy and so rich he that wouldn't have time to worry about the constant pain his spirit was in."

"Anyway, after boot camp I attended a navy training school to become a Yeoman (executive secretary, office / human resource manager). In this position, I was more interested in the executive secretary position and less interested in the office manager/human resource positions; so I intended to work hard to earn a position as the personal assistant to the head of a department or even a high ranking officer. I was told in school that personal assistant positions were hard work and hard to come by, but also a lot of fun and very beneficial for my career. My ultimate goal was to work in the Spanish or German Embassies or at naval facilities located in Spanish or German speaking countries. When I graduated from high school, I was fluent in German but my Spanish still needed some work."

My plan was not to interrupt her, but my brain was trying to process where speaking German came from. I said "German" with a very puzzled look on my face.

"Yes, German!"

"Weird, huh!"

"I acquired a love of German in the ninth grade, when I met Evonya, a German immigrant. Evonya's father's company opened a division in South Carolina and he was transferred to help set up operations in my hometown. Right away, she and I figured out that we had many things in common. Her family was a Christian family, she was a vegetarian and I was working my way in that direction. We were in several classes together which, was a blessing for both of us. Evonya knew very little English when she arrived at our school, so I helped her learn her way around school, as well as, get her homework assignments."

"Evonya and I became best friends, while we taught each other our perspective native languages and protected each other from the fu-fu girls and guys in high school that thought it was entertaining to mispronounce our names or make jokes because we brought our lunch instead of eating what was served in the cafeteria. Even after all these years, I can still remember the horror of cafeteria food. YULK!!"

"Students made fun of us because we were quiet, reserved and very smart. Teachers would assign us projects together, which was great for Evonya, because I was more willing than others to take the time to explain what the teacher wanted us to do. It was good for me, because I didn't want to be bothered with the other students."

"Also, as we learned about each other, we discovered we were both Christian teens, which was rare in my school and we practiced the same faith. Although we attended different churches, we were able to participate in many youth activities together. This was very exciting for us, but especially Evonya because she left her church, school and her friends in Germany and feared coming to America would be devastating for her. I believe one of the reasons we did so well is because, at the time, we were as serious about our relationship with Jesus as we were about our education. Evonya and I remained friends throughout high school. Upon graduation from high school, Evonya's family moved back to Germany but we continued to keep in touch. Evonya became a bio-chemist and worked for the European Centre for Disease Prevention and Control. Over the years, we have visited each other when she was in the states or when I was in Europe. Actually, we will be going to visit her during the Christmas holidays for the wedding of her daughter."

"My Spanish, on the other hand, left a lot to be desired. I passed my classes with honors, but I still felt I was not ready to be a translator. My plan was to go to college after high school to study foreign language, literature and to become an interpreter, but after my mom died, I just wanted to leave. When I joined the Navy, I requested orders to any naval base in a Spanish speaking country. After I completed boot camp and yeoman training school, my first duty station was Roosevelt Roads Puerto Rico. Getting assigned to Puerto Rico was a dream come true for me, as if God dropped the perfect job in my lap."

Lizanne told me that her goal while she was in Puerto Rico was to strengthen her Spanish and when her tour was over to transfer to Germany. When her Navy career was finished, her plan was to use her tri-lingual status in her future career, whatever that was going to be, as an interpreter. Meeting a man was not on her list of important things to be concerned with. We ordered more drinks as she told me about how she and Antonio first met in the Navy so long ago...

"My first job in the Navy was as an executive secretary. My boss was Lieutenant Antonio Martin who was one of the department heads at Roosevelt Roads Naval station in Puerto Rico. He was an interpreter for the base commanding officer. My security clearance was such that, as his yeoman, I traveled with him to most meetings as his transcriber. In this capacity, I was able to fine tune my Spanish skills and travel. It was great that my boss was Hispanic because he would speak to me in Spanish, which helped me and aggravated some of the others working in the office. He was a great boss and I had the perfect job."

"As for a man, well ... Lt Martin, well ..." *she hesitated as she searched for the right words...* "he was Hispanic, he was a few years older than me and he was very nice looking ... actually he was very nice looking indeed, Hispanic – Bi-Racial – Puerto Rican mom and Black dad ... there were days when I had to pray those minute prayers for strength and endurance. MY ... MY ... MY ..." *she paused, kind of swished the ice in her glass with her finger and smiled and whispered ...* "he still is" *as she shook her head.*

"Anyway, he was very fine and nice but not really my type, not really someone I thought I would want to build a relationship with. He wasn't my type – he was actually kind of nerdy. Not short but not tall, nice build but not athletic – which I was. But most importantly, I did not see him as a man serious about his relationship with Christ. I could tell he had a Christian background, but he was what the old folks called "on the fence." And besides, it was basically illegal to fraternize, especially romantically, with officers, AND ESPECIALLY your boss, so, he was a great boss and that was enough for me. It never dawned on me that this early encounter would turn into something more substantial at a later date in our lives."

Again, she just kind of chuckled and shook her head... We looked at the clock. We had been sitting there for hours, just talking. The restaurant was about to close.

Lizanne had set goals for herself. Since she did not complete her associate's degree before joining the Navy, as soon as she was settled in her job she started college. She knew it would take a little longer because she was working fulltime and traveling with her boss, but she worked hard and eventually she did finish her associate degree. She was able to take some of her bachelor's classes, even though the school on base didn't have a full Foreign Language program. However, they did have a Literature program, so she made it work for her.

She had a few friends, but she really didn't have time for the "party over here and the party over there" crowd, it just wasn't her thing. On occasion, she had parties at her apartment where she could control who came and what was going on and many of her friends enjoyed her parties because it gave them a chance to really enjoy good conversation, play board games, eat good food and not have to worry about someone throwing up on them.

She preferred to maintain her identity as a Christian, because it was the only thing that held her together during her mother's illness and death. Her life had turned into pure crazy while her mother was sick. She watched her father almost die trying to care for her. It was difficult for her to hold on to her faith during this time. Her brother, however, lost all faith and caused even more problems for her and her father. In jest she would say that one of them had to stay saved, it might as well be her.

Lizanne and I met again at the same restaurant and we actually were able to get the same table we had before. In some mysterious way, I believe it helped to formulate the story. We ordered drinks (sweet tea), lunch and I allowed Lizanne to ponder where she wanted to start. She looked at me with a look of despair in her eyes...

CHAPTER FIVE
Meeting #4:
"Marcus Antonio Martin"

"Therefore a man (or woman) leaves their father and their mother and
embraces their spouse. They become one flesh."
(Paraphrased from Genesis 2:24 MSG)

"Well, I guess in order for you to understand why that restaurant scene was so crucial and what happened to get us there, you have to know the people that make up this lovely, dysfunctional family of mine. And, the best place to start is the Patriarch, Marcus Antonio Martin. I wish I had been able to meet Marguerite before she died. I only was able to spend a few years with Marcus before he died. He was a character. He loved his family. Unfortunately, the one he loved the most was the one that was never willing to recognize it. He was so full of anger and I believe Martin died from a broken heart. He had lost his beloved wife and his oldest son. I heard in a movie once that a mother is only as happy as her saddest child. I'm sure that goes for fathers as well."

Marcus and Marguerite were my husband's parents and they loved each other with a passion that you only read about in Harlequin romance novels. But, like romance novels, there is always tragedy and despair, then hot passionate love everlasting. Theirs was a marriage that people prayed for and never had a hope of enjoying – not even me.

One of Marcus Martin's boyhood dreams was to drive trucks. Big trucks cross country. He loved watching the trucks pass his house in Beaufort headed to the interstate. He wondered what it would feel like to ride in the cab of a big rig. Immediately after high school he got his wish. He enrolled in a six month truck-driver class at the vocational school. In this class he was able to receive a CDL Class B license which meant he could not drive the "big rigs" but he was able to get a job after school. He wanted to continue training for his class A certification but the Vietnam War was raging and about the same time he was about to be drafted into the military he found out he was going to be a father. He decided to join the Navy rather than be drafted into the Army or Marines, and of course, the recruiter promised him he could drive trucks in the Navy so he said ok.

He and his girlfriend, Phyllis, quickly married at the courthouse so that his baby and she would have benefits. He enlisted the next week and left for boot camp. Although Marcus' parents were disappointed in his circumstance they loved him still and supported him in any way they could. Phyllis' parents, however, were furious that she had 'gotten' herself pregnant and now ran off to marry a boy with no means of support. They were upstanding citizens in the community, as well as, in the church. Phyllis was a debutante destined to be a Delta like her mother. Her father was running for city council and this pregnancy was not only inconvenient, but also embarrassing for them. Abortion was definitely not an option which meant they had to endure the humiliation. The humiliation of their daughter's pregnancy was nowhere near as dreadful as her marrying this boy from 'over there someplace' with parents who were nobodies who probably didn't even belong to a church and certainly did not hold a position in the church or in the community. They hated him even more when he joined the Navy, leaving her there to basically "fend for her."

Phyllis's parents refused to accept the fact that Marcus was raised in a Christian home and continued to remain spiritually connected to God. He and Phyllis made a bad choice, but they wanted to make it right for them and for their child. Her parents did not know his plan was to complete his boot camp and technical training, return for his wife then move her to wherever the Navy sent him. Unfortunately, their marriage was doomed from the beginning. After six weeks of boot camp, he started training at Construction Mechanic School in Port Hueneme, California for eighteen weeks to learn equipment repair including gas and diesel engine repair. His wife stayed with her parents. He was able to go home for a short visit before leaving for his first duty station, a ship in San Diego, California. He made arrangements to take his wife with him to California. He had housing set up, everything was in order. But, her parents did not feel it was safe for her to travel and then to be so far away, with no one to help her. Her parents insisted she stay with them, as opposed to going into labor and delivering their grandbaby on a naval base in California. October 31, 1956 Marcus was riding a naval ship headed to somewhere in the Philippines to build a temporary base when his son was born. He knew he had a boy and assumed his name was Marcus, Jr. A month later, he received a picture of his son and wife and he found out that his son was not named after him at all. His wife named him Timothy Wade Martin, after her father, who did not have any sons, instead of after her husband who was her baby's father, Marcus. Marcus was not consulted; her parents convinced her that it wasn't important to name the child after Marcus because he chose to be overseas instead of with her. She went along with her parents. Her father was called Timothy so she decided to call him Wade. Marcus was very disappointed and angry, but he did not cause a scene. His son was healthy and he would have his family with him soon.

His son was six months old before he was able to see him for the first time. His wife was happy to see him, but distant. Her parents were slowly convincing her that marrying Marcus was really the worst thing she had ever done. And to top it all off, these "Christians" already had someone else in mind they thought would be a better husband for their daughter and father for their grandson. He was a Deacon in their church and much better suited for her. The only thing in the way was her trifling husband. They never tried to get to know Marcus or his parents whom they only met once or twice after Wade was born. They had gotten in the habit of referring to him as trifling so much that they hardly ever used his name. Her parents would say to their relatives and friends "That trifling son-in-law of ours … "I will NEVER understand why she married that trifling-no count boy." "He's never going to amount to anything." They refuse to acknowledge that Marcus was doing very well and advancing in the Navy.

As he grew older, the most harmful thing Phyllis's parents did to ruin the relationship between Marcus and his son was to belittle him to others in front of Wade. At this point, he was basically the sperm donor and check writer, even though they ignored the fact that he paid all of his wife and sons expenses. Nevertheless, they made a point to poison Marcus in the heart and spirit of their daughter. Marcus was able to transfer to Norfolk, Virginia and again he had arranged for base housing for him and his family. She moved to Norfolk with him, but it was really too late for his marriage. After two years, they both realized their marriage was terminally broken. Wade was five years old. She moved back with her parents, filed for a divorce and Marcus moved into the barracks on base, with the other single men.

Marcus prayed for his son daily and spoke to him as often as possible, because he couldn't be with him and he felt that his ex-wife and her parents made a grave mistake separating him from his son. Her parents continued to bad-mouth him in front of Wade. The few times that he was able to visit them in South Carolina, it became more and more difficult to spend quality time with him, except at his parents' house whom Wade did not get to spend much time with because Phyllis did not make arrangements for them to spend time with him. He was beginning to believe the terrible things that were said about his father and his father's family.

Within a year of their divorce Phyllis married the man her parents preferred. Within a few months of married his company relocated and they moved to a small town about 100 miles from Charleston. Despite everything, Marcus maintained a relationship with his son, which caused interference in the relationship between Wade and his step-father. Phyllis's new husband and her parents wanted nothing to do with Marcus or his family, although they continued to cash the checks he sent every month. When they moved away it was easier to keep Wade from Marcus parents. As Wade got older, there was less and less communication between them. Phyllis never called Marcus. Her husband didn't allow it and when Marcus called Wade was asleep, outside, at practice but never available to talk to his father. He continued to send support, birthday and Christmas for him, but sometimes he didn't even receive a thank-you from Wade or Phyllis.

Even though Wade was only six years old when his mother and stepfather married, he knew that he did not like his stepfather, that he was afraid of him and that he and his mother were not treated right. Whenever Wade tried to talk to his mother or her parents about the abuse, they dismissed his concerns. He did get a chance to tell Marcus' parents about how unhappy he was and when they called Phyllis, their concerns were explained away as a boy vs step-father issue, not abuse of any kind. At one point, Phyllis allowed her parents to scold Wade and told him he was ungrateful and that he should appreciate having a "real" father. His grandfather mentioned the complaints to Wade's step-father which made it harder for Wade and Phyllis. Phyllis parents were so blind with status and money that they ignored the fact that they had put their daughter and their grandson's life in danger.

Marcus parents contacted him about the abuse Wade told them of. Marcus was finally able to talk to Wade and his mother only to find out that this perfect man was indeed an abusive husband and a neglectful father. He was very upset to find out that, due to her husband's abuse, Phyllis was beginning to neglect Wade's physical and emotional needs. When Marcus called Phyllis's parents, they were insulted that he would accuse them of ignoring the complaints of his son and Phyllis.

Phyllis was afraid of her father and husband, and therefore continued to defend her husband, refused to leave him and refused to allow Wade to move with Marcus's parents. She chose to continue to live in fear, with her life and her son's life continually in jeopardy.

Marcus petitioned the courts and the Navy for full custody of Wade. Because he was a single man and in the military, he was denied custody. His parents were denied due to their age and illness. Whenever possible, Marcus had his local friends and family check on Wade. He also brought Wade to visit in Norfolk whenever possible. Marcus worked really hard to protect his son as much as he could. Despite all of Marcus' efforts, Wade was scarred by the abuse of his stepfather and neglect of his mother. He blamed everyone for his misery, including Marcus.

Deep down Marcus knew that he and Phyllis should have never been together and after they became pregnant he just wanted to do the right thing by her and the baby. Now seven years later

Marcus was very disturbed by what was happening to his son, both physically and mentally. He knew Wade blamed him and the other adults in his life. Marcus tried to assure Wade that he was not going to leave him unprotected. But he was distressed because he knew it would be difficult to get his son away from the horrible conditions he was forced to live in.

Marcus tried to be a good dad, however, the barriers were astronomical. Because of his job, he was separated from Wade and now he and Wade were a statistic – Black marriage failed – Black man not in his son's life – Black fatherless son. In the darkness of his room, for the first time since this madness started, Marcus cried and he begged God to help him keep his son safe.

Marcus continued to trust in the Lord. He went to church whenever he could and he prayed that God would send him the wife that was truly for him.

After his divorce, Marcus requested early transferred, but that didn't happen right away, which actually turned out to be a good thing because he was able to spend time with Wade and his parents.

Two years after the divorce, he transferred to Roosevelt Roads, Puerto Rico. Wade was now eight and he did not take the move very well, especially when he realize that he could not go with his dad. Marcus was very concerned about leaving his son with Phyllis and her husband, however, he had no choice. His parents and friends said they would keep up with him.

Another Christmas, in another country, far away from his son. He tried to call, but no response. He sent gifts before he left the States, but he didn't know if they arrived. When he finally got through to Phyllis, her husband answered the phone said they were sitting for dinner and Wade wasn't able to talk. As Marcus was telling him he was calling from overseas, which of course the man already knew, the call disconnected. Marcus could not believe it, the man hung up on him. At that moment he knew for sure that his son was not in a safe place and there was nothing he could do about it right now.

By now Lizanne and I had been talking for about five hours. We told the bartender we'd see him in a couple days, same table... same time. He waved us off and we went outside. The night air was warm but cool, perfect for a spring evening. Neither of us said anything for a minute, just taking in the surroundings. We hugged, said see you on Thursday and went our separate ways.

I went home, poured another Moscato, and sat down, turned on my recorder and began to review everything she had said for the last four hours. I'm thinking this is only the beginning. I can't even imagine what will happen next. I wondered about Lizanne and what has been going on in her home lately. She is not about to give me a hint and I don't know how much longer I could wait to find out. Well patience is a virtue and I don't want to be like the curious cat! I smiled, turned off the lights and went to bed.

We met on Thursday. I had just come from an interview with the newspaper about my previous book and book signing schedule. The journalist tried to trick me into revealing something about my new book, but I told him "no, no, no you have to wait like everyone else!" Anyway, I was dressed like a grown-up - dark suit... dark shoes... in other words quite boring; while Lizanne, on the other hand, was dressed to compliment the beautiful spring day it was. The temperature was about 80 degrees. Living in Beaufort was great because we actually live on Port Royal Island. Regardless of how hot it is, there is always a breeze. Anyway, she had on a long flowy sundress that was multiple shades of orange, yellow and green. It fit her bodice but flared from the hips down. It had lacy shoulder straps which matched the lace around her waist and near the tail of the dress. This particular day, the only reason there was a breeze was to compliment her dress that flowed in the direction the breeze chose to send it, as if to bring the world to attention, to show homage to the queen. Her braids were held back by an orange scarf with yellow flowers. She had on a simple pair of orange sandals and she carried an orange purse. She was quite stunning, and I know this because every man on the street and in the restaurant was drooling at the sight of her and every women, including me, was horrified at the thought that we will never be that beautiful. As for me, I looked like her secret service agent or secretary or something so no one paid me any attention.

Our usual table was occupied, so we had to sit in a different section of the restaurant. It was a nice seat, away from the crowd so we could talk. We ordered and while we were waiting for our tea, she said that her husband was ill, so she didn't know how long she could stay. If she gets a call she would have to leave. For no particular reason she said that she knows so much detail about her husband's parents and siblings, because between them all, they had told her the entire story of their family which helped her to understand her husband, Antonio and his brother Wade better. She paused for a couple seconds and continued to talk about Marcus.

I mentioned to her that she was talking about Marcus' transfer to Puerto Rico.

CHAPTER SIX
Meeting # 5:
"Prayers Answered"

Marcus was relieved to be removed from the daily reminder of his broken marriage. He couldn't help but worry about Wade, especially after the encounters he had with Wade's step-father which were always negative and confrontational.

Marcus was finally able to talk to his Wade on New Year's Day. When he called his parents, Phyllis had allowed Wade to visit them while she was visiting her parents. Again the conversation he had with Wade was unnerving. To pour salt in the wound, Wade told him that his step-father decided he did not deserve presents and did not want to give him the presents his dad and grandparents sent him. Phyllis gave him the presents anyway and as a results his step-father was very angry with his mom. Again, Wade wanted to move in with his dad or his grandparents. Marcus said he would try, although he knew it was not as easy as that.

Marcus first Christmas holiday in Puerto Rico was okay. He hung out with some of the other single sailors and ate dinner in the chow hall on base. The other men went into town, but he didn't. Since he planned to go to church the next day, he decided it would be best to stay sober. So he stayed in and watched a football game, at least the parts he didn't sleep through.

The second week he was in Puerto Rico, he walked up to the counter in the exchange and saw the most beautiful women he had ever seen. He could not get her out of his mind ... her soft features, her almond colored skin, her brown hair pulled back in a ponytail, her beautiful smile and eyes like onyx stones. He wanted to fall into those eyes and live there forever. That day he saw his true soul mate. That day he was sure he heard in his spirit that she was his wife. When he left the exchange he couldn't get her out of his mind. He went back just to see her but to his dismay… she wasn't there. He went every day for a few days, hoping to see her, but no luck.

The following week he had to go away with his team for a month. The whole time he was gone, he tried to keep her vivid in his mind and prayed that she would be there when he returned. As soon as he was back on station he went to the exchange; well actually he took a shower and changed clothe first. Even though she did not know him, Marcus wanted to look his best when he saw her again. And there she was a bright light in a dark world – at least that was what she was for him.

From the first moment he saw her, he loved her and he knew that his prayers were answered. She would always be the perfect woman for him. Every time he went to the exchange, he would make sure he stood at her counter. Sometimes, all he purchased was a pack of gum or a pencil because he just wanted to see her. She soon realized that he was at her counter all the time. She would smile at him and ring up his one pencil, but she did not say anything to him outside of what was necessary for the purchase. One day, he got up enough nerve to ask her name. She looked at him, as if she was contemplating whether she was ready to be so revealing to him, or that maybe it was time to call security. After what seemed like ages, she said "My name is Marguerite Hernandez. What is yours?" He told her his name was Marcus Antonio Martin. She smiled and motioned to help the next customer. He left. He continued this routine for several weeks until he got up enough nerve to finally ask her out to dinner. She agreed to go out with him and they started to see each other on a regular basic. He was smitten, and soon enough, so was she. She eventually felt secure enough in him to allow him to meet her family. He learned Spanish to communicate with her family, especially her father. After courting her for a year he finally got up enough nerve to ask her father, in Spanish, if he could marry her. Although his street Spanish was enough to get by, it took him a month of tutoring from her brother to learn the proper way to ask for Marguerite's hand.

"Señor Hernández, me encanta tu hija con cada fibra de mi cuerpo. ¿Por favor me bendiga con el honor de permitirme formular Señorita Marguerite si ella sería mi esposa?"

Which in English says, Sir, I love your daughter with every fiber in my body.
Would you please bless me with the honor of allowing me to ask Miss Marguerite if she would be my wife?"

Of course her father pretended to give him a hard time, but her family already loved him and he was happy to give his blessings. So, after all that she had no choice but to say yes.

In the 1960s military personnel had to have permission to marry anyone. The approval of the request was at the discretion of the commanding officer, which could be good or bad. His current commanding officer was known to be against interracial marriage. Marcus prayed that God would bless him. His request was denied. Marcus resubmitted his request. It was denied again.

He told the Lord that if Naaman could dip in the Jordan River seven times, then he could submit his request seven times if that is what He required him to do. He reminded God that he would be transferring back to the mainland in a year and he would have to start the process all over again, which could take years. He also reminded God that he and Marguerite promised they would keep their courtship pure until He gave them permission to marry, which they did and now the only thing between him and his wife was the Jordan River. He didn't have to wait seven times.

He submitted his request the third time. God had transferred the commanding officer that denied his request twice. The new commanding officer immediately approved his request once he saw that Marcus had submitted his request three times. Marcus was due to transfer back to the mainland right before Christmas.

Marcus and Marguerite set their wedding date for June. 1967. Marcus' parents and Wade traveled to Puerto Rico. Marcus was very happy Phyllis allowed Wade to come, even though her parents and her husband wanted to disagree. However, since Marcus paid for everything they had no say in the matter. This was his parents' first opportunity to travel outside of the United States and to meet their new daughter-in-law.

It was a great opportunity for Wade to spend time with his dad and to meet Marguerite and his new family, especially his new grandparents. They all loved on him more than he had ever known in his life.

Marcus and Marguerite had a traditional Hispanic outdoor wedding at her parent's home.

When Marcus saw his bride walking towards him his eyes started to water and he couldn't hold back the tears. She was so beautiful in the white satin dress her mother and grandmother made and the veil Marcus 'mother made for her. Her dress was covered with beautiful hand embroidered lace and her veil was also hand embroidered with the same lace. What Marcus didn't realize was that Marguerite was trying her best not to tear up and ruin her makeup, but when she saw Marcus in his dress white Cracker Jacks, she couldn't help herself. She just kept thanking God for the blessing He was bestowing upon her. She vowed to God that, with His guidance, she would be the best wife possible. When she reached Marcus he wanted to just touch her to make sure he wasn't dreaming… that this day was all real.

The wedding was beautiful and the reception lasted into the night. Wade had never had so much fun around grownups. There were so many children his age. They all spoke Spanish and he didn't but they seem to get along just fine. At one point he found his dad and hugged him very tight and then ran back to play with his new aunts, uncles and cousins… an experience he never had at home.

Marcus was trying to contain himself, however, all he could think about was that this beautiful woman was his wife and soon he would be able to make love to her for the first time, because he had chosen to honor her by waiting until they were married. That day had come. His parents stayed for a week to enjoy their vacation and get to know their new daughter-in-law and her family. Wade was not worried about staying with his grandparents. He already loved Marcus parents and now he has new grandparents that already loved him… unlike his mother's parents who never loved on him.

Marcus and Marguerite chose to honeymoon at the hotel near the Naval Base. They wanted to save money to move Marguerite when he transferred to his new duty station. They honeymooned and spent time with their family before his parents and Wade had to leave.

CHAPTER SEVEN
"A New Beginning"...

Marcus received orders in transferring him and Marguerite to Jacksonville, FL in January, 1968. However he was heavy with grief because he had to leave her behind until housing was available. His heart was broken and he felt waves of anxiety as the memory of his last marriage flooded his mind and the problems the separation caused. But, God had given him a wise wife and Marguerite was able to calm his nerves and help him to understand that they were forever and he did not have to worry. The icing on the cake was that once she arrived in Jacksonville, they will be having a baby. It took him a minute or so to comprehend what she was saying. When the light bulb blinked, he was dancing in the floor. He was going to be a dad… again. He praised God for giving him a second chance at love and at being a father. Housing became available and Marguerite was able to join Marcus in March. They were never separated again. She gave birth to their first TWO children on April 19, 1968. They were both shocked and then ecstatic. They named their twins Maria and Antonio. What a blessing.

Wade was not named after Marcus but after his ex-wife's father, so Marcus wanted this son to be named after both of his grandfather's instead of after himself; so he was named Antonio, after his father and Luis, after Marguerite's father.

Wade was twelve. He was not as happy as his dad and Marguerite. As it was, he had very little time to spend with his dad. Now he had to share his dad with TWO other children.

Marguerite started school in America eventually receiving a degree in accounting and became an accountant for the Navy Exchange. She was able to transfer her position to the Navy Exchange at every naval base he was transferred to. During his career, although he never was stationed there again, they traveled back to Puerto Rico for vacations several times so that all the children were able to have a relationship with her family.

CHAPTER EIGHT
"Recruiter's Don't Lie"

The recruiter did not lie. Marcus did drive trucks. He also became a master truck mechanic. He was able to learn more about trucks and trucking companies than he anticipated. Marcus had a very successful career. In 1969 he was promoted and transferred to become an instructor in the construction mechanic school in Port Hueneme, California where his career first started. Along with his family, Marcus was also granted permission to take Wade, age 13, with him to California for the three years they were stationed there. This was a very good move for him and for Wade, as well as an opportunity for Wade to have a true relationship with his sisters and brother. Marguerite and Marcus' third child, Esabelle, was born while they were in California. Considering Wade wasn't used to having babies around 24/7, he did okay as a big brother. He also was beginning to realize that his Dad really did love him, really did want him and really did want the best for him. He learned that being angry all the time wasn't going to change the past or help him progress into the future. When Marcus and his family left California, they were transferred to Marcus' hometown of Beaufort, South Carolina, to complete his final years before retirement. Although Marcus was totally against it, Wade's mother insisted that he return to live with her and to finish his last year of high school at home. Her decision proved to be Wade's downfall.

In 1977, the year before he retired from the Navy, he purchased a trucking company that was in bankruptcy and closing down. Marcus opened his own trucking company, MMTrucking, Inc. As part of the settlement he retained the trucks and equipment,

as well as drivers and staff. He also acquired several of the contracts, so in essence, he immediately had a working and functional company. As much as possible he chose to hire truck drivers that were military veterans with truck driving or maintenance experience.

Lizanne leaned over the table to whisper as if it were a secret..."" MM" stands for Marcus and Marguerite." She laughed and said it took folks years to figure that out. They wanted the name of the company to represent their family.

After serving twenty-two years, Marcus retired from the Navy in 1978. After a "respectable" amount of time for rest and relaxation. He continued working. He taught truck driving classes part time at the vocational school he graduated from. This was his way of giving back by helping young men and women realize their true potential. Marguerite continued to be his partner, only now, she was the lead accountant for their business, which was probably why he didn't lose his shirt on a couple of occasions when he didn't read the fine print. She was his backbone in every way.

Wade's last couple of years in high school was turbulent, at best. Even though her parents were the reason Phyllis and Marcus divorced and the reason, Phyllis and Wade were abused in every way by her second husband, they still did not like Marcus and they proved to be loving grandparents for Wade. He missed his other grandparents a lot. He was happiest during the times he was able to visit Beaufort or Puerto Rico.

Phyllis' parents continued to be a poor example of what it meant to be Christ-like. Their negative attitude towards Marcus and their lack of affection towards Wade, assisted in Wade's negative attitude towards God. Their attitude towards Marcus continued to be negative to the point that they refused recognize that he was still a God fearing Christian man; or that because of his faith he was a successful military man, husband and father. Her parents had not wanted Wade to go to California with Marcus, but for once, Phyllis did not give them a say in the matter, so there was no way for them to stop her from allowing him to go with Marcus. They were very displeased to hear all of the great things Marcus and Wade had done together, especially traveling back and forth to Puerto Rico.

As soon as Wade stepped through the door into Phyllis parent's house, he felt miserable, as if the house sucked the sun right out of his body. He shut down and eventually started gravitating towards his old friends. He tutored a little "nerdy" kid who talked about Jesus all the time, which got on his nerves. However, he liked the kid and his family. He made decent money from tutoring him so he endured the weekly visits.

Nevertheless, he was always two steps from being arrested and going to juvenile detention. Somehow, he always managed to have clean hands when his "friends" were being arrested. He would often have unsolicited episodes of explosive anger and paranoia with no explanation of what is wrong or how to fix it. He was hot-headed and would not listen to logic, especially from the adults in his life. Marcus spent as much time with Wade as he could. Wade looked forward to the times he went to Beaufort. The atmosphere was like night and day. So it made sense that when it was time for Wade to graduate from high school, he asked his dad if he could come to stay with him. Of course Marcus and Marguerite said yes! Marcus felt that if Wade was with him, going to school and working alongside him at MMTrucking, Wade would straighten himself out. As the oldest child, Wade could someday take over the business, along with his younger brother, Antonio and his sisters, Maria and Isabelle. Marcus also hoped that this would give Wade and Antonio another opportunity to build a solid relationship. Marcus felt that as an adult Wade would be able to reason things from an adult standpoint and change his attitude towards Antonio.

Wade was jealous of the relationship between his father and Antonio. He felt that his father favored Antonio over him. The more Marcus tried to reassure him that his beliefs were not true the more paranoid Wade was that he had been replaced by a skinny little "half-and-half." As the oldest, Wade felt he should have privileges that would never be offered to Antonio. What was amazing about the entire situation was that Antonio loved his big-brother. He wanted to be around him and hang out with him, as much as he was allowed and regardless of the fact that Wade, most of the time, was mean to him and would call him names like "half-and-half." As time moved on, the jealousy and anxiety Wade felt continued to grow into paranoia. A scary phenomenon began to occur. Wade was hearing 'voices' in his head. The voices were not always legible, but he knew that, whatever this was, it wasn't good. However, he did not tell anyone. He did not want them to "put him away". He was positive everyone would forget about him. Wade's jealousy proved to be detrimental for everyone, including himself.

"Anger is cruel and fury overwhelming, but who can stand before jealousy?"
Proverbs 27:4

We stopped, because Lizanne received the call she was expecting. She said she would call me to set another date to continue but right then she had to go see to her husband. We hugged and I told her I would be praying for her and Antonio. Antonio had a very rough several days so we didn't meet for about a week.

CHAPTER NINE

Meeting #6:

"MMTrucking, Inc"

Wade's mother wanted him to attend the local college. However, Wade was 18 and had already made up his mind to move to Beaufort where, in a couple years, he could start working with his dad a trucking business. He applied and was accepted into a technical school to earn a degree in Mechanics eventually getting his truck driving certification and license so he could drive trucks when his father's trucking company, MMTrucking, Inc opened in about three years. While in school, Marcus helped him get a job on base at the commissary assisting customers with their groceries. This job was perfect for any student. Wade was able to make his own schedule and the tips were always very good.

By the time MMTrucking was ready to start rolling, Wade had completed his school and was driving for a local furniture rental company. Marcus hired him full time. He started him driving small trucks with short day routes. He would on occasion allow Wade to ride with other drivers on long hauls, as long as there were two licensed drivers. At the age of 23, after a few months of probation, Wade was able to drive as the second driver on local and long distance routes. After a year, Marcus gave him his first truck assignments driving long hauls between South Carolina and northern routes such as Norfolk, Philadelphia, and Detroit. For several years everything about the business was going well. Marcus was proud of his oldest son and Wade was enjoying his job. He especially loved that he did not have to live with his half-siblings. The girls, Esabelle and Maria, were tolerable, but, Antonio was annoying. Honor roll, top of this … top of that. Jesus this, Jesus that. Wade took every assignment available just to get away from Antonio and to prove to his father that he was genuine about being a part of the family business.

Before they could turn around good, ten years had passed and the business was thriving. Marcus had brought in several long term contracts, both civil and government. The training school had become the "go to" school for drivers and companies up and down the east coast. The student attendance had reached about 150 students per year. Marcus and Marguerite were very pleased with their investment.

Wade was doing very well. He had been on the road as the lead driver for few years, which helped him to stay out of trouble and work hard. Marcus was pleased and started plans to teach him every aspect of the managing responsibilities of the company, as well as the school so that one day the entire business would be turned over to him and Antonio. Marcus was looking forward to retirement and living out the rest of his years with Marguerite. Antonio joined the Navy, so he was not involved in the mechanics of the business, except as a silent partner. But deep down inside, it did not sit well with Wade that he would share the business with his *half*-brother. Quickly, he allowed the anger and jealousy of his childhood to return.

Wade learned the function of the various departments very quickly. Marcus promoted Wade to the operations manager over dispatch, all of the drivers and shipping, as well as, an operating budget. Not including drivers, Wade had a staff of five people (secretary, bookkeeper, contracts administrator and two maintenance supervisors) who helped him with the day-to-day operation of the department. Wade's responsibilities included: maintaining the budget for the operations department; managing the drivers, dispatchers, training/hiring/firing of drivers, maintenance of the trucks; training and verifying certification of drivers that were not trained by them, making sure truck route were not compromised; and ensuring shipping and contract regulations were followed. Marcus personally mentored Wade, sent him to a leadership training course, and taught him everything he needed to know to be a successful manager. Wade had all the tools he needed to be a successful manager and supervisor.

Giving Wade this responsibility afforded Marcus the opportunity to spend more time with Marguerite and to concentrate on the training school. Unfortunately, Marcus was not able to discern that although Wade loved his father, wanted to please him and be successful in the business, his ulterior motive still was to prevent Antonio from having any authority in the business. Marcus also did not know about the "voices".

Marcus was a Godly man and he prided himself on how he interacted with his family and how he instilled the importance of Godly behavior in his business. He did not require his employees to go to church, or even be Christians, that was their choice. However there was a certain decorum he expected from his employees while representing him and his company. But Wade did not have that same viewpoint. He still wanted nothing to do with God. He allowed Satan to feed dishonorable ideas and his selfish motives for having more control of the business. Although he knew that his father's ultimate plan was to give him and Antonio the business when he retired, he did not want to wait that long to get what he wanted. He refused to share his position with anyone, especially Antonio. His plan was to take and keep what he thought was his regardless of how it would hurt his father along with everyone in the family.

While Marcus was so proud of his son's accomplishments, his son was planning to steal the entire business from him and Antonio or cripple it trying. On one day, his wish came true and on another day he ruined everything, for himself and his father.

CHAPTER TEN

Because Wade was doing so well, Marcus no longer felt he needed to closely manage his performance. He loosened the reigns and gave Wade the freedom to do his job without constant supervision.

Marcus was very worried about Antonio. He felt Antonio needed a visit from his parents because he was going through a rough moment.

Of all the children, Antonio was the closet to his parents.

Antonio and his sisters were raised bi-lingual which came in very handy when Antonio decided to join the Navy, becoming an interpreter. Yes, he followed in his father's footsteps and joined the Navy after graduating college and becoming a commissioned officer. Antonio studied hard in college, graduated summa cum laude with a 4.0 GPA and was selected as the salutatorian. He missed being valedictorian by 1.45th of a point. His father was very proud pinning on Antonio's ensign insignia and given the honor of being the first enlisted service member to salute him. His family was very happy to learn his first duty station would be in Puerto Rico. During this tour he enjoyed spending time with his family, really learning about the maternal side of his family as well as becoming fluent in Spanish. He met many people whom he was honored to serve with, including his wife, Jasmine, a navy nurse.

Jasmine was second generation Cuban-American from Bronx, New York.. Antonio was in the hospital after being injured in a motorcycle accident. Jasmine was one of his nurses during the ten days he was hospitalized. His parents came to the hospital when they received the news of his accident and she overheard him speaking to his mother in Spanish. His mother was fussing at him for being reckless while continually calling him "Papito" which was her term of endearment for him. He begged her not to call him that in public... "Mommie por favor, si le oía llamarme Papito aquí, se empiezan a llamarme Papito de la Lieutenant (Mommie please, if they hear you call me Papito here, they will start to call me Lieutenant Papito)." She ignored him and Marcus just shook his head and laughed.

Jasmine was not fluent but she was able to understand some of what he and his mother were talking about. When his parents left, Nurse Jasmine would call him Lieutenant. Papito'. He was furious but what could he do, he was broken and Nurse Jasmine healed him. In 1991, he and Jasmine married. They remained married for eight years until she filed for a divorce due to "irreconcilable differences."

Unlike Antonio, Jasmine was not dedicated to the Navy. She did not want to travel with him and eventually she did not want to remain in a marriage with him. At the time of their divorce, they had two children, twins age six, Antonio Jr. (AJ) and Alondra. He was devastated. He thought they would be together forever, raising their children together, like his parents. Jasmine didn't have the luxury of growing up in a "whole" family and so it was easy for her to walk away from the marriage once it no longer suited her. She wanted out of the marriage and when she filed for the divorce she was already in a relationship with someone else.

Antonio loved his children very much and they thought he was the best dad ever. When he learned of the affair he considered filing for full custody of his children. After considering his work and travel schedule he decided against it because he knew he would not be able to be a quality fulltime custodial parent. As a result he reluctantly allowed them to remain with their mother but maintained joint custody with the option that at any time they could come to live with him if they chose to do so.

At the time of the divorce Jasmine and Antonio were living in Charleston, South Carolina. Jasmine considered relocating closer to her family in New York; however, she chose to stay in Charleston due to her position as head nurse at one of the hospitals in Charleston, as well as the children could remain in their school and maintain their relationship with their grandparents who lived in Beaufort, South Carolina.

After the divorce Antonio plunged into his work as a means of ignoring how devastated he was. Fortunately for him, his work afforded him the ability to travel all over the world. As a result AJ and Alondra became world travelers. Several times they visited his family in Puerto Rico, as well as, wherever he was stationed, including Japan and Russia. It was a great experience for them.

Otherwise, outside of work, Antonio chose to spend time with his family and friends, but he had no intent on getting romantically involved with another woman any time soon. Like his dad, deep down he knew his relationship with Jasmine was failing and probably should have never happened in the first place. However, he felt if he prayed enough and tried to please her that she would stay. It just wasn't to be. So Marcus and Marguerite went to spend some time with Antonio, which left Wade unattended and thinking he is in charge of MMTrucking.

CHAPTER ELEVEN
"Wade 'In Charge'" ...

Slowly Wade began taking advantage of his position. Within a year he walked around with a "boss attitude" but he was not doing the work of a manager or leader. Wade was continually cancelling department meetings and unprepared when he attended managers meetings. He was not allotting time for mandatory upgrade training for any of the drivers, even though he was reminded on several occasions of certification deadlines.

For a while, Wade had begun to imagine "voices", other than his own, talking to him and given him "advice" about how to handle different situations in his life. He still refused to tell his dad or anyone about these voices. Several of the "recommendations", Wade felt, were very beneficial in his quest to take over MMTrucking. There was one standing practice since the inception of the company that Wade adamantly disagreed with which involved recertification of the drivers. Wade knew the contracts guaranteed if the driver paid for their class and recertification fee, MMTrucking would give them the week required for school with full pay and benefits. The voice asked, "Why should *we* pay them money they did not earn."

Since Wade disagreed with paying the drivers for time not spent on the road, instead of addressing his concerns with Marcus, he chose to ignore the requirement for recertification. He even told a long standing driver that he was easier replaced by younger drivers. This driver and several others approached Marcus with their concerns because their certifications were about to expire. When questioned, Wade's first excuse was he had a lot on his plate and forgot. He told Marcus he felt since the drivers were responsible for paying for their license recertification they should be proactive enough to get their training on their off time. Why should company pay for them to be off of the road while they are in class? He felt they should not be on the clock while in school and he (Wade) was changing the policy – although he had no authority to do such a thing. Marcus was furious, but he couldn't deal with Wade's attitude right now. He had to take care of his drivers. Marcus arranged and paid for the certification classes and licenses for the drivers that were immediately in jeopardy. He then set up classes for the other drivers as needed. All of the drivers in jeopardy were paid time and a half while in school.

Marcus began to wonder what other policy "changes" Wade decided to make during his absence, so he thought it beneficial to review and inspect everything that Wade was responsible for. Immediately, Marcus notices the schedule of one of the drivers. Several months earlier Wade hired three drivers, Thomas Harris, Hezekiah Jackson and Christopher Gregory, with questionable backgrounds in an effort to "give them a break" similar to what his father gave him. The men were not acquainted with each other, but for various reason they had difficulty getting hired by other companies.

Although fully qualified and meet all of the required mandates to drive trucks short and long distance, Marcus' stipulation to hiring the three drivers was that they be closely supervised for six months and that they would not be able to drive alone for one year. After one year, if they proved themselves, they would have a truck and routes of their own. Without dispute Wade and the drivers understood and accepted these perimeters. Just one thing though, Wade did not disclose to Marcus that Christopher Gregory and he were "associates" from his hometown, back in the day and that Christopher was fired from his last company for drug use.

At the end of the first six months Wade took Chris out of restricted status and gave him a truck of his own without supervision. Harris and Jackson remained in a supervised status but did not question Wade's decision nor immediately report to Marcus what Wade had done.

By the time Marcus discovered the noncompliance of his directions, Chris had made three solo trips. One more thing to argue with Wade about, but now Marcus was beginning to see a pattern of Wade defying every directive from him.

And then, the pot exploded. On Chris's fourth trip he was pulled over for speeding on the interstate. The policeman asked for his credentials and his license. His partner was running the tags to get information on the truck. The problem was that Wade had not done his homework well. Chris had outstanding warrants... more than one... one of which was a serious offense. When the officers returned to the truck Chris could see that this was not going to be a good day.

When the officers asked Chris to step out of the truck, he became very agitated. By now other police had arrived. As a result of the warrants, he was immediately taken into custody. Because he was acting suspicious the cab of his truck was searched. The police found two handgun magazines under the passenger seat of the truck. After a further search of the cab the police found a concealed weapon. Chris did not have a license for a concealed weapon. Chris's problems imploded when one of the back-up police cars was a K-9 unit that just happened to be in the area at the time of the call. The police dog alerted near the rear of Chris's truck giving the officers probable cause to search the entire truck, inside and out. The K-9 unit opened the trailer and found boxed with the legal merchandise large quantities of both cocaine and marijuana.

While the search was in process, Marcus, not Wade, was notified by the highway patrol that one of his trucks had been seized and the driver arrested. This is how Marcus found out that the driver was carrying and selling drugs across state lines while on his route. Wade immediately said he knew nothing about the warrants, drugs or the weapon, basically throwing Chris under the bus. This is how Marcus discovered that Wade was not maintaining proper records of any of the drivers' routes, including Chris' routes. Also found were various discrepancies in funds paid through his department. Wade blamed the discrepancies on the bookkeeper and when that didn't satisfy Marcus, the contracts and shipping administrator. It was easy enough for Wade to blame her because a month ago she noticed discrepancies between the reports Wade turned in and the receipts/invoices coming from contract companies. She mentioned these discrepancies to Wade several times with no explanation for how it happened or how to fix them. Wade actually accused her of purposefully making errors on the reports. What Wade didn't know was that she took her concerns to Marguerite who, after further verification presented the reports to Marcus. They reviewed all of Wade's records. Almost too late, Marcus realized that Wade was falsifying documents in every area he was responsible for and stealing from the company. Wade was using drugs, gambling and using the company as his personal bank account.

Marcus knew Wade was involved with Christopher Gregory but Wade made sure none of the transactions of the drug sales could be traced to him. So although Marcus suspected that Wade was involved, there was no tangible proof that he knew about transporting drugs or the weapon. During the trial, it was revealed that Chris and Wade were acquainted prior to his employment at MMTrucking. However, without proof, for now, Marcus had to take Wade's word. The trial for Chris was long. He was eventually charged, convicted and sent to prison for drug trafficking, in possession of a concealed weapon without a license and various other charges. He silently vowed to make Wade and MMTrucking pay for what they did to him.

In order to maintain his contracts and his drivers, Marcus had to regain the trust of his employees and the companies he contracted with. Fortunately, Wade's plans crashed before he had an opportunity to cause major damage to the entire business. Marcus chose to fire Wade rescind his driver's certification and license. He chose not to press charges for embezzlement and falsifying documents, but only if Wade agreed to rehabilitation for substance abuse and gambling. Marcus did not want to believe that his son would steal from him. He didn't want to send his son to prison. More importantly, Marcus began to realize that Wade's anger was damaging to himself and everyone else. And Marcus wondered, "Can all of this really be because of his dysfunctional childhood and did he truly dislike his brother Antonio so much that he would sabotage the entire family?" Wade had to choose between prison and rehabilitation. He chose rehabilitation. For a second Marcus wondered if his son may be suffering from a mental illness and what could be done to help him. However, just as quickly as that thought entered Marcus mind, it left.

He remained in rehabilitation for six months. During those six months, he was diagnosed with paranoid schizophrenia and bi-polar disorder. He did not give the doctors permission to reveal this information to his family. After Wade completed rehabilitation his doctor continued psychotherapy and writing his prescriptions. He also promised not to tell his family as long as he remained in therapy. Wade agreed.

CHAPTER TWELVE
Meeting #7:
"MMTrucking Restored"

Marcus and Marguerite started repairing the damage Wade caused. They held recertification classes for all of the drivers, even if their credentials weren't due. The drivers that could not recertify were fired and new drivers hired. The blessing occurred when, because of MMTrucking and Marcus' reputation and moral ethics prior to Wade's tenure, the affected contract companies agreed to remain with the company as long as Wade was not in charge of their contracts. Within a year, MMTrucking was back on its feet providing quality service to its customers.

After rehabilitation, Marcus reluctantly hired Wade as a dispatcher, but would not allow him to drive or be responsible for maintaining or reviewing reports or contracts. The stipulation that Wade be gainfully employed and supervised was the only reason Marcus agreed to rehire him. He was also required to pay restitution to MMTrucking and retest for his personal driver's license.

A few weeks after Wade was released from rehab, he was severely injured in what everyone thought was a random mugging. However, Wade knew who sent those men after him and why; he also knew that it wasn't over.

After one year of what seemed to be a clean sober life Marcus sent Wade to school to recertify and regain his trucking certification, but he did not hire him as a fulltime driver. He did it to show the other drivers that he was not showing favoritism to his son by bringing him back without the same training and certification requirements that was required of them. He wanted to be fair to his drivers and to his son. Since Wade seemed, to be in his element as a driver, Marcus put him back in a truck as a substitute driver doing local and short runs. He eventually gave Wade a northern route, which for the moment, satisfied Wade because he could drive as much as possible. It seemed to everyone that he was maintaining his sobriety and getting on the right track again.

Little did Marcus know, throughout all of this, Marguerite was dying. And his son was again plotting how to use company money to pay for his current drug and gambling debts, as well as the debt had accrued before he went into rehabilitation, which included the cost of the drugs confiscated when Chris was arrested.

Wade continued to use drugs because the medication from his doctor was not enough to quiet the 'voices' in his head and the pain in his spirit.

CHAPTER THIRTEEN
"Marguerite"

Marcus' beloved Marguerite was diagnosed with cancer. Their daughters lived nearby. Their youngest daughter, Esabelle was a nurse, which was a great help in caring for Marguerite. Antonio was in the Navy overseas and Wade was driving more and more. Wade spent time with her when he was in town. Through it all, he loved Marguerite. She treated him the way a mother should treat her child, which was more than he ever received from his own mother. Even though it was the early 1990s, cancer was still a mystery and early diagnosis was rare. After intensive chemotherapy Marguerite went into remission for a year.

Then, the cancer returned. Marcus did everything he could to love his wife back to health. His daughters were more worried about him than their mother. Both of their parents were senior citizens and his health was not the best. Marguerite was a devout Christian. She had made her peace with God; she was fine with the possibility of death. They bought a hospital bed big enough for him to lay with her. On days when she was in the worst pain, he would wrap his arms around her as much as her body could handle and would sing to her one of their favorite songs; a song he learned in Puerto Rico. She laughed as much as she could because he had the worst frog voice in the world. Throughout their marriage, he would always sing to her when she was having a moment and she always loved him and his frog voice even more.

Besame, besame mucho,
Como si fuera esta noche la última vez,
Besame, besame mucho,

Que tengo miedo a perderte, perderte despues
"Kiss Me ... Kiss Me a Lot,

As if tonight were the last time,

Kiss Me ... Kiss Me a Lot,

For I have fear of losing you ... losing you afterwards ..."

Marguerite's only regret was not being able to cuddle up next to her sailor like she was used to before she became so ill. On days when it was too much for him to bear, she would wake up to find him in tears with his head on the bed. She would touch him, telling him that everything will be alright. She would then sing "Besame Mucho" to him:

"Quiero sentirte muy cerca mirarme en tus ojos verte junto a mí
Piensa que tal vez mañana yo ya estare lejos, muy lejos de ti"

"I want to feel very close to you... look in your eyes... see you next to me

... For tomorrow I will already be far, very far away from you."

Before she became ill, Marguerite taught Maria, her eldest daughter, everything about the finances of the business. Maria had become an accountant with a desire to work in the family business. Marcus did not have to worry about business as he had very good managers for the company and school.

Antonio come home on emergency leave to visit with his mother, before she died. He took her illness and death the hardest. First, because he could not do anything to help her or make her better, but mainly because he was her only son and when life got hard he could always call his mom. Now, when she needed him, he could not help her.

But for Marguerite, he was her Papito, always would be, even though he was married and had given her beautiful grandchildren. Most of all, she knew that he loved his mother dearly. When he thought about it, he was glad that she had been able to live a very beautiful and joyous life, which included, coming to visit with him at his various duty stations. She assured him that she had no regrets - because God had blessed her beyond measure. She told her children and her husband, "continue to live your life as if it's your last day. Love God with all your heart, with all your soul, with all of your strength and He will bless you. And we will all be together one day in heaven with Him." No one wanted to cry, but they did... tears of sadness but also tears of joy.

One sunny day, August 20, 2004, Marguerite wanted to sit on the porch and listen to the birds sing good morning to her. Marcus sat on the rocker with her, holding her in his arms. She was feeling quite weak and her voice had become very frail, but she wanted to talk to him for a little bit. She told him how grateful she was that he took his time to introduce himself to her in the exchange. She laugh as she told him the only reason she married him was because he asked her father for her hand in Spanish. She told him that she was grateful for the beautiful children, including Wade, that he gave her. She thanked him for MMTrucking. MMTrucking had truly been an adventure. She told him that loving him had been the joy of her life. She told him to take care of the family, including Wade... even in his illness, he will figure it all out one day. She told him to keep his hands in God's hands and they will be together again sooner than later. He kissed her on her forehead and then she closed her eyes. The love of Marcus' life left him. Marguerite died in Marcus arms. He held her until there was no more energy in her. She was the spark that ignited him daily; she was the smile on his face; she was warmth he felt whenever he was cold. How could he continue on without her? He cried until there were no more tears left in him. Maria was pulling into the driveway when she saw them on the porch and she thought it looked like old times. But when she walked up the steps she could see her father's tears. She knew her mother was gone. She was so overwhelmed she couldn't think for a moment, because even though you know the time is coming, you don't expect it when it is actually here. She called her husband, her sister and brothers. Esabelle and Wade came right away. Antonio had to fly in and didn't arrive until the next day.

Marguerite was buried in the Beaufort National Cemetery plot she and Marcus had purchased for the both of them. At the time, they assumed he would go first, but he buried her there first. Then, he went home, and laid on the bed she had occupied for so many months. Although he thought there were no more tears left, he cried some more.

CHAPTER FOURTEEN
"When there are no words... Hum"

After Marguerite died, the girls called to have the bed removed because they found Marcus sleeping in it a couple times. Marcus allowed the managers at the business to handle everything. He needed some time to breathe and to adjust to life without Marguerite. He use to tell his friends that he loved her before he knew who she was and she used to say that he was the man that she dreamed would be her mate for life. That the first day she saw him in the exchange she knew it was him, but she wouldn't tell him. She just waited and the rest was a storybook love affair. Marcus did what most spouses do, after his daughters and granddaughters took out pieces they wanted to keep, he packed her clothes to give to the church's community services team. Things he didn't want to deal with right then he boxed and put in the attic. Sometimes, he didn't do anything, just sat on the porch and watched the birds. Then one day, he decided he would live, even though he didn't know how without his Marguerite.

Marcus continued on with the business. He was happy that his daughters and grandchildren lived nearby because it helped him not miss his Marguerite so much. They also protected him from the church and neighborhood widows who thought it was their job to cook casseroles for him every day and show up to his house or business in their Sunday best dress on a Tuesday. After all, he was a young and very handsome sixty-seven year old man who owned his own business – the perfect catch. No matter how much he thanked them and told them he was fine and did not need them to continue to cook for him, they continued anyway. He stopped going to church potlucks because it became a competition, for the ladies, to see whose food he would eat. He didn't want to tell them that he took the dishes to the lunchroom at school for the students and drivers. Eventually, the pastor asked them to give him a break which prevented Maria from speaking to them "firmly" in English and Spanish.

MMTrucking was thriving again, but more and more Wade was becoming a topic of distress for Marcus and the business. He was missing deadlines or not showing up to work and there was clear evidence that he had started using drugs and possibly gambling again. He still wanted to keep Wade in the family business, but he could not see how that would be possible and he definitely could not give Wade a position where he would be responsible for any operation or financial function of the business.

About six months after Marguerite's death, Wade came to Marcus and told him that since he didn't trust him to run the business, he should give him his financial share of the business and he would leave MMTrucking and the family alone for good. Marcus again, tried to reason with Wade but he did not want to hear anything being said and as he was arguing with his father, Marcus suffered a heart attack. Maria kept asking him was he trying to kill her father. She yelled at him, "Why can't he just be happy? Wade kept saying he didn't do anything wrong. He was just trying to talk to him. He wasn't trying to kill his father. For a moment Wade really was worried that he had pushed Marcus too far. He knew he wasn't being respectful to Marcus and he knew he was causing much distress for him and the family, but he didn't expect him to have a heart attack. But before he could ask Marcus or God for forgiveness the 'voices' told him he shouldn't care because if Marcus died, than he'll get everything. Wade cursed at the thought, but did not accept his actions as part of the reason for Marcus' heart attack.

Marcus recovered from the heart attack and although he was only sixty-seven years old, his body was not healing quickly because he was still mourning Marguerite, and actually thought he might get to be with her sooner than later. He also continued to work instead of giving himself time to recover from the heart attack, because he would not trust Wade to handle the business. Wade did care that his step-mother had just recently died, but her death had nothing to do with his rights to the business. He cared that his father was sick. However, his major concern was that he needed more money to cover ongoing drug and gambling debts which were becoming a problem for him; so in his mind he had reason to resent Marcus, because he would not turn the business over to him or give him his own revolving expense account. He resented Maria because she was worse than her mother when it came to keeping a close eye on the business finances, what money going out and what money that was coming in. But most of all, he resented his younger brother because he knew that Antonio was about to retire from the Navy and would become the new CEO of MMTrucking.

In 2005 Antonio was being considered for a promotion and a command position which would take him out of the country and away from his teenage children for a long period of time. Leaving them at this point in their lives was not an option. He had a full, successful career that he was proud of and although he could see him staying for another ten years, he made the decision to retire so that he would be available to his children and his aging father. He needed to be near his father because his mother had just passed away and his father's health was weakening. The Navy had been a great adventure for him but it was time for a new adventure ... MMTrucking

In 2006 Lieutenant Commander Antonio Martin retired from the United States Navy after twenty years of honorable service. At his retirement ceremony he was commended for his dedicated service by many people. But the biggest honor was that his father, his sisters and his children were there to celebrate with him. He felt a twinge of regret because Wade refused to attend. Over the years, he had come to realize that, no matter what he did, his brother had no love for him.

CHAPTER FIFTEEN
Meeting #8:
"Antonio Luis Martin"

So of course, Antonio retired in Beaufort, SC so that he could be near his children and one grandchild, one hour and thirty-four minutes away and where he could work with his dad who should have retired years ago. Antonio was not anxious to confront Wade. He was no longer the little skinny "half-and-half" and he wanted answers. Wade knew what had transpired between him and his father and why his father never retired in order to save the business; but Antonio didn't know the entire story. He didn't know that Wade was the cause of his father's heart attack. He did not know the full extent of Wade's drug and gambling abuse and exactly how much he had stolen from the company. While in the Navy his father chose not to tell him everything. Maria told him the entire truth and showed him the records and told him that Wade was a boiling pot that needed to be watched very closely.

Throughout his Navy career, Antonio was a silent partner. However, he was well aware of the operation of both the school and the trucking company. Marcus just had to help him become acclimated to how the businesses were run. What the standard operating procedures (SOP) were. Antonio spent time meeting with the department heads and the employees, getting to know them and familiarizing himself with how each department was operated. Many of the leaders and employees loved their jobs and Marcus. Some have worked at MMTrucking from the day the doors opened. The department heads did tell him about the problems Wade had caused, especially, with the drivers and the shipping department. They felt really bad that Marcus had to cut him but they understood. Sometimes blood is just not enough.

A year after he retired from the Navy, Antonio took over as CEO of MMTrucking and School. Marcus officially retired but he remained President of the Board and Antonio's mentor. It was a great celebration for everyone, except Wade.

Although Marcus was against Antonio retiring earlier than he had planned in order to care for him and the business, Antonio's return home actually put a little pep in Marcus step. They spent a lot of time together doing things that retired people do… fishing… fishing… and oh yeah… fishing. They tried to persuade Wade to join them. He spent time with them once or twice just to save face. He was not interested in being chummy with neither his dad nor his brother.

In 2015, Marcus died from a massive heart attack and was buried with his beloved Marguerite in the Beaufort National Cemetery. Marcus would say his only regret in life was Wade's refusal to acknowledge that he loved him and has always tried to take care of him and protect him. Although Wade wanted to blame his misery on others, he never admitted that he was destroying his own life. No matter how much Marcus prayed for his son and talked to him over the years, Wade never wanted to accept how much Marcus and his brother loved him.

Antonio inherited MMTrucking Company, instead of his older step-brother. At his father's recommendation, Antonio refused to give Wade a partnership in the business but did allow him to maintain his job as driver. Needless to say there was dissension between the two brothers which later became a very big problem for Antonio and MMTrucking.

Lizanne was very solemn when we met today. She said "I know I'm jumping around but today was a good day to talk about my first husband, Chef James Robert McKenzie, U. S. Navy, Retired.

Today would have been our anniversary."

CHAPTER SIXTEEN
Meeting #9:
"Feed me till I want no more ... "

I've been telling you all about the Martins. Today is an anniversary I observe in solitude. When I still lived in Puerto Rico, all of my other-than-work experiences while in the Navy was, to say the least, bland. I had friends and fun. I enjoyed the island of Puerto Rico. There was always something interesting to do, to discover.

One of those discoveries was James McKenzie, Head Chef for the base Admiral. Everyone called him Chef Jay. This was James's second tour in Puerto Rico. He was coming close to his ten year mark in the Navy. He was a well-known executive chef and the Admiral he's working with would be headed to Washington DC as her next assignment in two years and she planned to take him with her. His goal was to retire and to open a restaurant in Washington DC, which is his hometown, so returning to Puerto Rico turned out to be a win-win situation for him and the Admiral.

One day while catering a luncheon, "he saw the most beautiful young woman he had ever seen"- at least that's the story he told our son whenever they talked about how he and I met. He would say when he saw me he knew I was the real reason he was back in Puerto Rico. He was going around asking everyone who I was and when he found out I was a Yeoman he asked the Yeoman on his staff to find out who I was. Just by luck, one of them went to my bible study class. So what does he do? He joined the class. To tell the truth, even though he was most definitely tall, dark chocolate handsome, I had no eyes for him because he was several years older than me and it was obvious that he had no clue which part of the bible was the front. But, since I am southern breed, I was hospitable and I helped him with his bible study. As time went on, he actually became very interested in what he was learning and he was able to ask me to spend more time with him studying. I had to laugh because he figured out the way to my heart was the studies, not his good looks nor the fact that he could cook!

Chef Jay had never married. He used to joke that the Navy was his wife and no women could replace her. But meeting me definitely changed his perspective of marriage tremendously. He was an old man, compared to the sailors I hung out with; so he had to work hard to gain my affections, but once he did, I was head over heels for him. We fell in love and on April 6, 1979 we were married. The wedding was beautiful. My father was retired from the ministry, but he was still able to officiate. Even my brother, Justin, came to the wedding. I was really surprised to see him. He and James hit it off right away, again surprised. We honeymooned in St Thomas for two whole weeks. It was wonderful.

A little more than a year later we left beautiful Puerto Rico. I changed my career plans to accommodate my husband's plans. Instead of transferring to Germany, I transferred to Washington DC to be with James, as well as to complete my master's degree. I decided to devote my time to my husband and all the children we planned to have.

We were married for 15 years. We had one son – JR age 13, one daughter – Tia age 11. I was pregnant with a "surprise" baby on the way. We were living the Hallmark movie life. I was working in a government office in Washington DC as an interpreter; James retired from the Navy in 1984 and opened what became a very prestigious restaurant.

All was well with my world until August 15ᵗʰ, 1994, when my husband was killed by a drunk driver while we were visiting my family in Detroit, Michigan. The drunk driver did not notice that he was driving on the wrong side of the street at an ungodly speed, and therefore did not realize he had hit another car. He did not realize that the father in the car was killed, that his thirteen year old son was severely injured and that his wife, who luckily was not in the car, was eight months pregnant with their third child.

She paused for a bit, took a deep breath and sipped on her tea in order to gain her composure.

All the men went to a game. I thought they stopped for pizza or something which is why they were late getting back in. Tia and I stayed in because I wasn't feeling well. At my age and eight months pregnant I was having minor difficulties so I decided to stay home to get some rest. When the doorbell rang I just assumed it was them with their arms full. When I saw the policemen I collapsed before they could even say anything. Even though we were visiting relatives, my spirit knew they came because of James or JR. They knew where to come because they were able to retrieve the registration of the car he was driving. Luckily my cousin had just stopped by to visit.

In an instant the love of my life, my king, my counsel, my soul-mate, my best friend was gone. The last time I saw him, he said "see you later and love you more" which was what he always said when he left my presence, even if it was just to go to the backyard. In an instant my entire life had been destroyed.

I rushed to the hospital to see about my son, praising God he was still alive. The extent of his injuries made it touch-and-go for a while. Then I had to go to the morgue to identify my husband.

Tears begin to flow but she continued on...

My cousin went with me, which was a good thing as I collapsed again. The doctor said the impact broke his neck and he died instantly. As a gesture of condolence, the doctor said "he felt no pain." How can doctors know whether there is or is not pain?" I wanted to ask if James knew he was dying; of course the doctor wouldn't know that. Only God would know that and right now, I didn't want to talk to God. So one more time, I had to bury my family. Even with God's help, how was I to endure such a tragedy.

My life forever changed, I questioned God's motives for continually allowing these tragic trials in my life. I yelled at God one day for continually taking from me! How could He allow my husband to be killed in such a manner? Why would He take him from me? Wasn't my mother enough for Him? Why was it important to allow the trifling driver to live - the drunk who was always on the edge of Hell! My husband loved God. He was full of life, enjoying us, his son, his daughter and his restaurant. He was looking forward to our new child. We had decided not to find out the gender. Although we were hoping for a girl, we decided since God surprised us with another child at our age, He could surprise us with the gender of our new child at birth. Why would God allow a drunk driver to deny James the ability to see his new child? Or cause JR to possibly not be able to fulfill the dreams he had in life if he was disabled as a result of the accident? *But you know what I really wanted to know?"* "Why would God take Tia's father, at the age of eleven, just like he took Justin's mother when he was twelve?" I worried that Tia's faith might be challenged as Justin's was and still is. I had to work hard to help her keep her faith in a God that allowed her father to be killed and the murderer to live!" After my mother died, it took all I had to maintain my faith and love for God and my spiritual standing. When my husband was killed, my faith was under attack and the attacker was winning.

The moment I recovered from the initial shock of the accident I called my dad and Justin. They both came immediately. This tragedy brought a beginning of healing for my dad, my brother and me. On the morning of the funeral, I sat in my kitchen trying to drink a cup of Earl Grey. I asked God if James' death was a means of mending my family. Is this the window that has opened because James' door was shut?

Three days after the funeral, I went into labor. At first I thought it was just pains caused by stress, but soon I realized it wasn't. My dad and Justin were still with me and rushed me to the hospital. Twelve hours later, Jamie was born. Two months premature but very healthy. The doctor said she guessed Jamie felt she could be of better service to her family outside than in. Jamie's birth was a blessed event… a rainbow after the storm.

The drunk driver that killed James did not know any of the facts surrounding the accident because his car did not stop until he hit a tree on the other side of the street and was broken and unconscious. He was severely injured and placed in a drug-induced coma. Within a week or so he regained consciousness and was informed what he had done. While in the hospital it was discovered that he had several prior incidences of drunk driving and even destruction of private property. He was arrested and convicted of vehicular homicide. He was only sentenced to five years in prison. My husband's life, my son's livelihood was only worth five years to the Michigan justice system. When I walked out of the courtroom, I knew I would never be the same again… it was a devastating state of affairs.

Once everything about the funeral, the birth of Jamie, the rehabilitation of JR and the trial was over, I had to learn how to function on my own without James. I was now mother and father for my children. Some things became mechanical for me. I hired a very close friend and colleague of James's to manage our restaurant and it continued to run smoothly and to make money. At first I never wanted to set foot in the restaurant again, but JR and Tia wanted to go. I would have relatives take them. Eventually I decided to visit and it wasn't terrible. I considered selling our beautiful home. That was for my comfort; I knew it would not be right to uproot JR from his school and friends. Also, we were around the corner from my mother-in-law, which was a great help to me, especially with Jamie.

I went back to work and basically used it in the place of therapy… as my drug of choice. I continued to go to church, unfortunately, my spirit was damaged. I soon changed churches because I could see my husband in and out of the building. It was just too much for us. The new church was just that … a new church. Like most teenagers, it didn't take JR and Tia long to become acclimated. No one knew me, except as "JR and Tia's mom." For the moment that was fine with me.

Too my surprise, Justin took a leave of absence and stayed with us for quite a while. He was a God-sent. I think if it had not been for him, I would have locked myself in my room and never came out. My little brother was no longer "little".

CHAPTER SEVENTEEN

Meeting #10:

"A Step Away from God"

"The first step away from God is to walk away from the people of God and the church."

Justin's college days were a fair share of academics, parties and non-prescription, not over the counter drug use. He no longer attended church on Sabbath or Sunday. Once he was in college, he felt he could handle his new lifestyle. He had no intent of going back home or to jail; he was much smarter now. College helped him stay focused on his grades. His goal was to earn internships that would help him achieve his ultimate goal - a career with a prestigious accounting firm. It was important that he graduate with at least a 3.5 grade point average and honors, which would put him in a higher standing for acceptance into graduate school. He had goals, despite the hypocrites.

He knew a lot of young women in college, though he avoided having real romantic relationships. Although very successful in academics, he was still fighting demons from his past, mainly denial, anger and unforgiveness. These emotions prevented Justin from truly allowing himself to formulate a real relationship with anyone, not even his family, so real relationships were not his cup of tea. Justin, my father and I stayed in contact on birthday, holidays and major family events. In actuality, the last time he spoke to either of us was in Detroit when our grandmother passed away. When our mother died he shut himself off, refusing to allow himself to care about anyone... sometimes not even about himself. He had no desire to accept anyone and refused to become vulnerable to anyone. He preferred to see women on occasion, when necessary, and with no strings attached.

He certainly did not talk to women that were in any form or fashion religious. As far as he was concerned God was a dead subject and he had no time to waste discussing Him, choosing instead to focus on much more pleasurable activities.

And then there was Grace. Justin met her at the library. She was so beautiful. Her skin was a perfect shade of dark and her locks fell in her face as her head was bent reading. He was thinking about which lines he would use first to get her attention, when he realize that at that moment she wasn't reading, she was praying, "UGHHH!!!, RIDICULOUS." He was about to walk away when she looked up. He was staring into her brown eyes, as deep as the universe itself. She spoke, he spoke. She smiled then looked at the papers in front of her. He just stood there. He knew he wanted to run in the other direction. *"He told me his feet would not move from the spot they were in."* All he could do was continue to look at her. She looked up at him again, smiled, and said nothing. Finally he had to say something, so he asked her if he could sit at her table, as if the library was completely full with no other seats available. She said yes. He sat across from her so that he could look at her beautiful face. He pulled out the first book his hand touch in his bag – Taxation. He then noticed she was not reading a text book. Once his eyes focused on what she was reading, he cursed under his breath. It was a bible and some lesson books. He recognized both. Now there was a battle going on inside him and every neurotransmitter in his brain was sending messages all over his body. GET UP! – RUN! – DON'T RUN! – YES! RUN AND DON'T LOOK BACK! He just sat there because his spirit would not allow him to get up. Not only was this woman religious, but he knew her faith and she would have a trillion questions about why he left God and the church.

Before he realized what he was saying, he told her he recognized what she was studying. She smiled and then frowned. She saw what looked like distress in his face. Inside, he was in distress and kicking himself for saying anything. He didn't want to talk to her about that. He wanted to see how long it would take to get her to agree to go out with him. Church girls pretend to be "saved" but get a beer or two in them and WHOO-HOO! PAYDAY! No, he did not want to talk to her about her church lessons.

She wondered if she really wanted to know, but she asked him why it bothered him that he recognized the books. His brain was saying to tell her it was nothing and then change the subject. His voice told her that he used to believe in God and study the bible and the books, but not anymore. He told her that even though he was raised in a Christian home he stopped attending church when he moved to college. She listened intently as he told her how he stopped communicating with God shortly after his mother passed. He could not believe he was blurting his story, this part of his life he has not spoken to anyone about, to a girl he did not know, and felt comfortable doing it. He explained to her how he gave up on God because God gave up on him. He was nine years old when his mother was sick. He prayed, he promised, he begged God not to take his mother. God ignored him and when he was twelve God allowed his mother to die anyway. All those years he watched his mother suffer, get better and then suffer more. God allowed her to suffer and then He allowed her to die when He knew how much he needed his mother. He was too young to be without a mother, God didn't care.

He paused. Justin began to feel the pain and agony he felt then. She said nothing. He wanted to stop talking. He couldn't. Something about her made him feel safe, so he continued.

God didn't care that there was no one to raise him. His father was so full of grief he paid no attention to him at all. His sister was struggling herself and joined the Navy the day after she graduated from high school. He almost hated her for not blaming God for taking their mother.

All of a sudden, he realized that she had not spoken a word while he told his story. She wasn't damning him to hell or anything like that. So, he continued to tell her that even when he continued getting into trouble. God didn't do anything to help him. When he was in detention, God did not protect him from rivals who threatened and harassed him daily. Now he was an adult and surviving just fine without God's help and he didn't need anyone trying to make him accept God. Then he stopped talking.

She still did not say a word. After a moment or two, she told him that she understood clearly how he felt. He was about to say something to her when he noticed the tears on her face. He was horrified but still arrogant enough to think that she felt it important to cry over his pain. Just as he was about to protest her tears she told him her story. Almost identical, except she didn't go to detention. She had to figure out that no matter how much pain she felt because of her lost, the pain she felt from turning her back on God was worse. She felt God deserted her and that her lost was due to her sins. So she abandoned God, not the other way around. She was miserable and discontent with her life. She considered suicide and would have succeeded had someone not found her. She said someone told her that God did not abandon her and that He would never leave her nor forsake her; that her fears were implanted in her thoughts by Satan, not by God. That day she renewed her relationship with God and the journey has been most pleasant. She told Justin she had to learn that it's the fault of the humans in our life that weren't there when we needed them... not God's fault.

He had no words. He actually thought he was going to be sick. After a long moment of silence, he stood up, picked up his books and said that he was about to be late for a class. He did have class, but he really wanted to leave, run and erase her from his mind. Instead he reached out and took her hand into his and said to her, "My name is Justin Webster. Maybe I'll see you here tomorrow." She said "okay."

He walked away trying to figure out what just happened. Did he make a library date with a religious chick? Impossible! He decided he was not going back to the library. But he did, many times afterwards, meeting with Grace. They debated the issues of God. While Justin enjoyed his conversations with her, he had no desire to attend church, commit to God, or to Grace. And to make sure there was no confusion, he told her he liked getting high and no human or God was worth quitting, at least not right now.

But midway through his sophomore year he realized honors and marijuana didn't mix. He chose honors, and even though he didn't want to admit it, he wanted to choose Grace. His spirit was telling him not to lose her, but his brain wasn't listening.

During winter break, he found a way to detach himself from her, for a bit, because he was offered a short-term internship at an accounting firm in Detroit Michigan. Instead of spending Christmas Break with his father, he accepted the internship. Justin's father, Pastor Webster, was okay with this plan as he had relatives in Detroit, which meant he wasn't totally alone. Although, it would not have mattered in the least. Grace was very proud of him for landing the internship and also for clearing the air, so that his brain cells could breathe.

He enjoyed working for this firm. They seemed to like him and his work ethic. He worked hard and learned as much as he could in the short amount of time available. He thought of Grace. He *almost* thanked God for meeting her; for such a perfect opportunity, but he caught himself. He accounted this success to his hard work and good grades. When his internship ended, the director of his department (corporate taxes) expressed how pleased he was with Justin's work and zeal for the business. He told him it was his intent, if he wanted it, to offer him a summer internship. Justin was overwhelmed. He accepted the offer. He was extremely grateful for the opportunity and learning experience.

Before returning to school, he went home to spend a few days with his father, which was about all they could stomach of each other. They had seen each other about six months ago for JR's birthday. Neither of them felt bad seeing each other for only a few days. He even went to church with his dad to see how the hypocrites were doing. Although Justin was making successful decisions about his career, his father would not accept that church was not currently in his plans. As a result, their relationship continued to suffer… basically stuck in neutral.

After being clean for several months, Justin decided it was a good idea to stay clean, concentrate fully on his school work, internships and career. He was awarded internships at the same firm for the summer and for the winter breaks of his senior year.

The one thing that disappointed him about this summer break was that Grace graduated and would not be returning in August. They promised to keep in touch. That never works out.

During spring break of his senior year he received an offer for a position at the Detroit firm. He was ecstatic. Again despite it all Justin graduated with honors. His life was moving forward and God had nothing to do with it – so he wanted to think. What he forgot was that God is longsuffering.

He moved to Detroit, living with relatives until he was able to get his own place. The firm he was employed by was housed in the world trade center in Detroit. He sat in his cubicle and laughed out loud wondering what those hypocritical nobodies are talking about now? What bad things can they say about him now – that he was successful – that on his first day of employment he was making more money, legally, than all of them collectively. He wondered if they cared that he was no longer using or that he was accepted into one of the most prestigious accounting Master's degree programs in the country. How can his father continue to have bad feelings towards him? He was moving on up and leaving them behind. Was he still not good enough for them simply because he had not returned to church?

To keep his father and sister from bugging him about going to church he maintained minimal required contact. His one regret was that he had lost contact with Grace. The last time he contacted her she was on her way to South Carolina to teach middle school. He wish he had kept in touch, but he really felt she was better off finding a man that thought the way she thought. The last note he received from her said that he was a prime example of people that believe they are justified by their works instead of their faith and trust in God. If he ever figured that out, he should call her He never called.

He did, on occasion, hear from Wade. They were friends on Facebook, but neither of them kept in close contact with each other anymore because their worlds were now so different. He remembered enough to know that Wade was in a very dark place and he didn't want to get involved.

CHAPTER EIGHTEEN
"Justin's Song: Praise is what I do ... even when I don't want to!"

"Since they didn't bother to acknowledge God, God quit bothering them and let them run loose. And then all hell broke loose..." (Romans 1:28 The Message)

Much to everyone's surprise, even his, Justin moved up in his company and was doing very well. Actually, he was doing a little bit too well. While very successful in his career, his personal life was a disaster. He still fought old demons. Although he gave up drugs in college, he eventually found alcohol to be his drug of choice. Alcohol was easy because it was legal and there was always a "drink to something" at his firm. He did not realize how dependent he had become on alcohol to numb the emotional pain he lived with constantly. It had become really easy to blame dad and me, and to blame God for his misery, but he knew it was all him.

Then the bottom really fell out. One morning, Justin came into his office a little early to do some final preparations for a new client meeting. When he arrived he found that his firm was in serious trouble with the federal government. The client he was scheduled to meet was somehow involved. The company had several "private" accounts that were not handled in the normal accountant rotations. Because of his stellar background in corporate taxes he was promoted to the department that handled special accounts. These were mainly accounts where the company's annual income was several million dollars. He had moved from a little fish in a big lake to a medium fish in a big pond. He was "moving on up!" as Mr. George Jefferson would say. Today was to be his first meeting with this client and he wanted to be prepared. Now people were scurrying from pillar to post and when he got to his office, he found his secretary in tears and government agents sitting at his desk.

The agents in his office informed him the owners and several other executives of his company had become entangled in stock and tax fraud. They were now in custody. Until further notice the entire firm had been shut down. There was also a potential threat that Justin and his team could also face prosecution because the clients involved had been passed to them. Justin was furious and then terrified at the thought of going to prison, especially for something he didn't do. So he did the only logical thing he could think of; he immediately called his big sister to be on the lookout for a good lawyer, if it came to that. He lived in Detroit and Lizanne lived in Washington DC. Nevertheless, he called his big sister for help.

As it turned out they didn't need a lawyer. Justin and his team kept immaculately detailed records. He learned in his policies class in college, better known as the "CYA class," to keep detailed records of every transaction to the point of being obsessive compulsive. In the beginning, Justin's team members were angry when he demanded they keep better detailed notes. That day they were grateful for his insistence of their attention to detail. He and his team were spared prosecution. Investigators realized they were able to prove, on paper, that they were not involved with the accounts or clients... clients they had not met. They helped the government rummage through the paperwork, identifying many such "accounts" and their discrepancies.

Legally he was cleared of any wrong doing. But, Justin knew one of the reasons they were spared was because his family and friends prayed for him. He still did not want to acknowledge God as his deliverer, but, in his spirit he knew that it was only God, answering the prayers of the saints. He knew of accountants and stock brokers who were framed and the big bosses went free while they went to jail, as well as losing everything. He wrote a letter to his sister and his father's church thanking them for their prayers on their behalves. As the letter dropped in the mailbox, he wondered what was happening to him. He could see Grace's smiling eyes looking at him over her glasses. Before this happened, he had not thought about her for quite some time. Justin wondered what was happening and what God had up his sleeve. Whatever it is, he is not interested!

His firm was court-ordered to pay the employees severance and maintain their benefits for one year. Justin was very dumb in some matters, but money wasn't one of them. He had several "legal pockets" of money located in various spots. If necessary, he could live comfortably for a while. After the dissolution of his firm, instead of going immediately to another firm, Justin admitted himself to an alcohol rehabilitation center in Detroit. He was so tired of being miserable. His professional life was on point, but his personal life was in despair. He needed peace without alcohol.

About midway into his program something very strange, but, familiar happened to him. He was emotionally drained after a private session talking about his mom, her death and how much he blamed God. Justin felt that God didn't care anything about her or him. He thought about Grace telling him she had to learn that God did not turn His back on her, but she turned her back on Him.

Before dinner, while sitting in his room trying to regain some composure out of nowhere he heard a small still voice saying, *"Justin, you left me but I'm still here. I haven't left and I never will."* Justin knew there was no one in the room but him. He knew who was talking to him. He knew it was the voice of his old friend, Jesus, and Jesus knew his mother taught him that verse when he was a young boy. He also remembered Grace quoting that scripture when she told him her story. Hebrews 13:5 *"…* for He will never leave you nor forsake you." But what Justin actually heard in his head was *"Justin, I will never leave You nor forsake You, no matter what you think of me."*

Justin was mortified at what he heard. He recognized that voice as the one he had conversations with as a child. He remembered the last time he heard the voice before his mother died. He remembered how he blamed God for everything bad in his life, even though he made the choices he made with no regard for family, God or even himself. He didn't want to hear His voice right then. He yelled at the top of his lungs, "GET OUT OF MY HEAD JESUS! WHERE WERE YOU WHEN I NEEDED YOU! The voice said, *"You need me now."* Justin broke down and cried like a twelve year old child that had just lost his mother. *"I hate you! I hate you for what you did to me,"* he said through his tears. But God said to him *"You hate me because your mom died; you blame me because you expected me to heal her. I did not neglect her, it was her time. I did not give her cancer but that is how she died. Yes you were only twelve years old, but I had everything in place for you, so that you would be properly cared for and continue to learn about me. But you chose the way you chose and although I never left you, I could not make you chose me. I have been waiting for an opportunity to tell you this, but I had to wait until you could hear me... until you were ready."*

Justin cried until he fell asleep. Hours later he woke still dressed in the same clothes from the day's activities. He was disoriented. He could not remember what day it was. Then he remembered the voice and his tears. *"WOW, what a weird dream,"* he thought to himself. But ... he knew it wasn't a dream, and he knew who was talking to him. *"Wow, I need to call Lizzie and tell her about this. It should make her day to know that not only is she tormenting me with "Jesus loves me still" but now He is chiming in with her."* Again he thought about Grace. He shook his head with just a little bit of disdain for God interrupting his moment of self - destruction.

Justin completed rehabilitation and was hired to work at another firm in Detroit. He loved Detroit and wanted to remain there. However, he soon lost his zeal for the city. He did not like working for the new firm. He was not happy, he was not content, and he barely existed. Oh, he had money, friends and prestige. All of the things he thought would make him happy and satisfied. But it didn't. Even though he had not lost everything, even though he wasn't eating with the pigs, nevertheless, he still felt like the biblical story of the prodigal son; and he felt the need to go home ... try to mend some fences.

For several years now, Justin and Lizanne had been in regular contact with each other. She had called him out of the blue and told him it was ridiculous that, even as a grown man, he would still hold grudges for what he knew was not her fault or their dad's fault. "Blame us for neglecting each other, but don't continue to blame us for mom's death." She also reminded him that he had a brother-in-law and a nephew who wanted a better relationship with him. After she finished chastising him, he told her he heard Jesus' voice.

When he told her about his episode, she didn't say any of the things he thought she would say. She called a little more often to check on him. Against his better judgment, and at her request, but mainly so that she would stop asking him, he woke up one Sabbath morning, got dressed and went to church. He did not stop for gas, or a newspaper or anything else that might distract him from going, because once or twice before he started out for church, but never made it. He went back once in a while, sat in the back and slipped out before the appeal and before anyone could ask him to stay for potluck dinner. But the real reason he slipped out early was because he didn't want anyone asking him if he had a church family, what he is doing and why he left the church in the first place. He was not interested in answering those questions, especially not with strangers.

About a year into his new job, a drunk driver killed his brother-in-law and severely injured his nephew in a car accident. Another reason to doubt God, Justin thought. God's intent was to kill his entire family. But at this moment, he told himself it wasn't about him. He took a leave of absence from his job to take care of his sister. He didn't want to be at work, so it was easy to leave his office and go to Washington DC. He was actually able to do most of his work remotely which satisfied his employers. Justin used this as a time to decide what the next transition in his career, and life, would be. He knew it would not be at this firm and probably, not in Detroit.

CHAPTER NINETEEN

Meeting # 11

"Like Esau and Jacob"

It was obvious to everyone that Wade and Antonio were not best buddies. It was also obvious that Wade was the reason. Even as an adult, Wade refused to let go of his jealousy of Antonio. Even after his father was buried, he still refused to give up his anger towards Antonio. After all, his birthright was being given to Antonio, his younger brother. He did not recognize that his hatred had denied him any type of relationship with anyone. He had no friends and his associates were drug dealers, gamblers and loan sharks. At this stage in his life, 50+ years old, most men would have grandchildren, but Wade never married and as far as he knew, he had no children. He never allowed himself the joy of a meaningful relationship with anyone. He used his energy to fuel his anger and conjure up schemes that continually made the family look bad. He was too narrow-minded to realize that he was just digging himself deeper and deeper into a hole he would not be able to pull himself out of.

Before he died, Marcus had begun to notice Wade's behavior becoming more sporadic; which helped him understand what Marguerite meant when she referred to Wade's "illness". Marcus did not know about Wade's "voices", but he knew something was wrong with his son.

Marcus' last verbal instruction before he died, which was reiterated in his will, was that Wade could keep his job as a driver as long he remained qualified. The ownership of the business and school would be divided equally amongst the four siblings; Wade would get his share of the business in the form of a monthly stipend from the company, basically, selling his shares back to the company.

A couple of years after Marcus retired from MMTrucking, he turned his home into a boarding home for single veterans and truck drivers. Each resident had their own room and were responsible for rent (utilities included) and their own phone. He always left one room unoccupied for Wade.

When Marcus made his will, it was stipulated that the home would remain a boarding house and that the tenants (or new tenants) would continue to reside there as long as they followed the rules and paid their rent. Wade's room continued to remain unoccupied until he needed it. The family was responsible for maintenance and yearly taxes.

Since Marguerite's death, Marcus had paid more attention to Wade and he begin to see a pattern that explain her last words about Wade, "even in his illness." Marcus asked Wade if he wanted to "see someone" about his anger. Of course, Wade got angry and said no.

Because of his suspicions, Marcus' most stringent stipulation of the will was that Wade should never be given controlling leverage, managerial control of the company or majority voting rights. As sad as it was, Marcus knew that if Wade had any leeway he would bankrupt the business.

At the reading of the will for the family and for the business, Wade was furious and he vowed that he would get what was due him. He stormed out of the meeting in a fury and did not come back to work for two weeks. His routes were shifted to other drivers so that contracts were met on time. Antonio, Maria and Esabelle met with lawyers, bankers and the board including department heads and stock holders, to make sure that Marcus' wishes were met to the letter, that their business and school was safe from outsiders trying to buy them out, but especially from Wade. Everyone now understood Wade did not care about the family, the business or the school. He only cared about what he could get and about revenge, even if that meant burning it to the ground.

When Wade returned, Antonio gave him the letters from the lawyers stipulating that he would no longer be an employee of MMTrucking, Inc, that he would receive a monthly stipend, as stipulated in the will, as well as stocks in the company, but that he would not have majority voting rights or a management position in the company. It boiled down to Wade receiving free money and having no responsibilities. Again, even though he brought this on himself, Wade was not satisfied.

MMTrucking continued to flourish under Antonio and Maria's management. Esabelle held a position as an owner and stock holder, but she enjoyed being a nurse and was not interested in the management and operation of the business or the school. Antonio hired a retired Navy colleague, Hank Anderson, with a background in training school management as the superintendent of the school which freed him from having to worry about both companies.

Although MMTrucking had always been successful, Marcus wasn't an expert when it came to upgrading the business into the computer age. He had computer technology installed, but not the best system, which continually provided opportunities for something to crash, for the company to be hacked or paperwork to be lost in "cyberspace." Antonio used his military background to help launch the business into the 21st century. While in the Navy Antonio had a buddy, Albert Monroe, from Charleston that was a computer, hard and software, wizard. Antonio knew that he had retired but didn't know if he was in Charleston. After a little bit of searching he found him in Charleston working for the Department of Homeland Security in dealing with cyber security. Albert agreed to help him install upgraded systems and work with him as a consultant. He also helped Antonio hire a fulltime manager for the computer / internet department and two technicians. Every department, including the school, received state of the art computer systems, as well as, training.

The school launched an online program for the in-class portion of the training, as well as training simulators. It was a big project and everyone was excited about the potential for growth to the company, even Wade. Wade spent his money as fast as it posted in his account. He lived way beyond his means. The 'voices' were tormenting him and he was really heavy into drugs now. The family knew he was deeper into drugs and continued to encourage him to return to rehabilitation. He refused. They did not know about the "voices."

In 2011, MMTrucking was invited to apply for a contract transporting government inventory. They would be transporting everything from pens and pencils to weapons, to commercial airports and shipping lines destined for deliver to overseas military bases. They already had ongoing contracts transporting to east coast military bases, but not national and definitely not with international destinations. It was a very intensive application process which included identifying specific drivers that would potentially be eligible for government clearance.

Six months after the application process was completed, Antonio received a letter stating that MMTrucking had received the contract. When he looked at the next two pages of requirements in order to complete the process he wasn't sure if he was happy or not. Maria was not happy when she saw that this account could not be mixed with the other company accounts but very happy when she realized the contract paid the salary and expenses to hire an accountant specifically for this account. In actuality, this contract would become its own department staffed with managers, administrative staff and its own drivers. The only dilemma was they only had three months to create positions and hire employees with approved government security clearances to stand up an entire department. Antonio had a video conference scheduled one month after the contract was awarded, at which time, he had to present their plans for the new department and the names of the potential employees who would qualify for government background security checks. MMTrucking completed the background checks normally required for hiring their employees. Fortunately, MMTrucking didn't have to pay for the government background checks which were extremely expensive. The highlight of this project was Antonio would travel to Washington DC to finalize the launching of the new department. He had friends in the area. He could actually use some down time... some social time outside of work and family.

At least once or twice Antonio thought about the fact that he was alone. He wondered if there would ever be another woman in his life that he would really be able to depend on, someone that would last for the long haul. Of course he'd had "dates" because his family, especially Maria, was always trying to fix him up with someone. None of the dates turned into anything potentially substantial and right now he didn't have time. He was busy with the business, his sisters' families, his children and their families, and of course, Wade. Although not active he attended his father's church, which he enjoyed. The Sunday morning music was good and the preaching was adequate, but he felt as if he needed more than what he was getting. He didn't know what the "more" was however, he knew it wasn't in that church.

And in the mist of everything, he needed a third eye to watch Wade who always seemed to be where he shouldn't be and falling deeper and deeper into his mess. He came to Antonio several months ago asking for a "loan" to pay a debt that was a problem for him. It turned out that Wade owed "bankers" in Charleston who were coming to "meet" him to collect their money. Antonio was very angry. He did not want to loan him the money but he did, so that he wouldn't have to bury him. Deep down inside he knew this would not be the last time Wade will need bailing out.

CHAPTER TWENTY
"How Long Lord ... How Long? ..."

One year... two years... three years. Lizanne's heart still hurt. She missed James and there was no one qualified to replace him. She attended the required functions of her job, family and church. She poured herself into JR who had recovered from the accident physically, but was battling with his own post-traumatic stress demons because of the accident. He would soon be old enough to drive, however, he had no desire to even test for his permit. He would say it's hard enough to ride, yet alone think about driving. He was preparing to start his junior year in high school. This would be the first year, since the accident, he would be mainstreaming back to a full day school schedule. Lizanne was grateful she was in an area where the academy was willing to work with her on JR's behalf. Fortunately, because of the extent of his injuries and the long period of time it took for him to regain mobility, he was able to continue his freshman and sophomore classes online, preventing him from falling behind in school. When necessary, she was able to transport him to the science and testing labs at the school, but he was not required to spend the entire day at school. Also, several of his friends studied with him at home, including a young lady who nominated herself as his personal tutor. This helped with his esteem and his post-traumatic stress.

Lizanne poured herself into Jamie because she was the gift God gave her when He took her husband away. Jamie brought joy and excitement into the house. It was impossible to be sad when she was around. Even so, there were times when Lizanne spoke only when spoken to and helped anyone that needed her help. But, personally, she was broken and she functioned in life as necessary, nothing more.

****

His wife left because their marriage was not important to her. He retired earlier than planned he wanted to spend time with his ailing father before it was too late. His mother passed while he was overseas; he could not spend those end days with her. Missing that time with his mother devastated him and he did not want to miss these last years with his father. His father truly needed him to help him with the family business because he was not as strong since his heart attacks. Had he not retired early, Antonio would have also missed time with his teenage children before they were too busy to have time for him. But, more importantly, at this point in his life, he had no personal life. He didn't even know if he ever wanted to consider marriage again. Although deep down inside he prayed the same prayer his dad told him he prayed - that God would soon send him the woman that was to be his true soul mate. In his mind he was about to be an old man. He remembered he had heard many times that God does have a sense of humor and He is not called "The Miracle Worker" for nothing. More important, he knows that He is always faithful.

CHAPTER TWENTY-ONE

Meeting 12:

"25+ years later"

We had not meet at our restaurant in a while, so we decided to meet there today. She wanted to meet for dinner. When she called I could sense that she really just needed to get out for a bit. I asked her how her husband was feeling these days. Her response was that he was "holding his own." She said he had some rough days, but the doctors seemed to feel that he was recovering as expected, especially since he would not stay away from work. She talked about how she and Antonio became reacquainted after twenty five years.

Tuesday morning at 9:13 a.m., August 16, 2011, we will never forget it. I was sitting in a conference room waiting for a virtual meeting to start. At this meeting I would start the contractual process with the chief executive officer of a privately-owned trucking company in South Carolina. The Navy had other contracts with this company. Although it made sense to continue to do business with them in this newest project as transport support within the United States, surrounding countries and internationally, the contract bidding process was long and it took some time before the contract was awarded to MMTrucking, Inc. The company had everything the contract required, but most importantly, the ability to transport anywhere in the United States and across the Canadian and Mexican boarders. The original owner, Mr. Marcus Martin, had grown his little trucking company into a multi-million dollar shipping industry and he had a very good relationship with government contracts and the previous liaison. I had not had the opportunity to meet with Mr. Marcus Martin before he retired. I would be meeting with the new owner, his son. While reviewing the contract, I thought the name seemed familiar, but I didn't really pay it any attention ... I mean for real, how many Antonio Martin's are there in the world... millions right!

The satellite engaged at 9:13 a.m. for a second, the image on the screen took my breath away. I was thinking "how did this happen." He recognized me immediately. "Lizanne McKenzie, is that you?" It was the voice of the ONLY Antonio Martin that I knew from twenty-something years ago. After all of these years, we just happened to show up in the same meeting. He and I looked toward the ceiling, "God you really have a sense of humor." We both had to laugh. It was a good thing the only other people in this particular meeting beside us, were our legal representatives and recorders. How the tables had turned. After all these years, I was now his partner.

After the initial shock of seeing each other, Antonio and I decided that when he came to Washington DC we would meet for dinner and catch up on what's been happening in our lives. Although he had to travel several times for contract structural meetings, we did not have time to have dinner or catch up. We wondered if God was somehow in the midst of us meeting again. How did it happen that we ran into each other now, and both of us are single? After all, we were at each other's weddings. It was just hard to understand what God was thinking. I was relieved that we didn't have time to hang out. We were both relieved we were 559 miles apart with less opportunity of rushing into something we might regret later.

Finally, after the completion of the contract requirements, we took time for dinner... mainly to celebrate the contract. He was very sorrowful to hear about James' death and I was very sorrowful to hear about his divorce. He knew my mom had passed before I met him in Puerto Rico he asked me about my dad and brother. I gave him the five-minute account of the life of the Webster's. I told him that although I had done a lot of research while my mother was sick, I was slow to recognize how much stress it caused my family, and how long after her death we suffered.

I told him that although I knew it wasn't her fault, deep down I felt my mother's illness ruined my family. Then when my husband was killed and my son temporarily disabled and now suffering from post-traumatic stress disorder, it was even harder for me. I was pregnant and responsible for caring for my son. Though I gladly nursed him back to life, it put a strain on me physically, mentally, socially but especially spiritually. I vowed that if I ever had such an illness I would not subject anyone to the type of stress of being a caregiver for me. I hope I would never be put in a situation like that again. I would be hard pressed to do it again.

When I said those words, I didn't know that one day we would be married. I didn't know he was paying attention and, most importantly, I didn't know I would regret saying them.

CHAPTER TWENTY-TWO
"You Can Always Go Home"

While helping Lizanne after the death of her husband, Justin came to the conclusion he couldn't effectively function in his job. He also didn't see his career expanding in this firm. He realized Detroit was no longer where he needed to be. Although he cringed at the thought, he felt he needed to go back to his beginnings and start fresh.

He chose to connect with a career coach, who really was only a recruiter for various head-hunter firms. He created a resume, completed a number of applications and posted his information on the various employment websites. There were several job postings in the Washington DC area but Lizanne told him she was considering moving home once JR graduated from high school. She advised Justin to move south. Their dad was elderly with dementia and it would be good to spend time with him before he dies.

One day, Justin saw a notice on an employment website for a lead accountant position in Beaufort, South Carolina, a small military town outside of Charleston, SC. The advertisement was posted by MMTrucking, INC. In the back of his mind, he remembered MMTrucking. It came to him... Wade Martin. He remembered Wade Marin's father owned MMTrucking. He did not want to be that "up close and personal" with Wade. As he was about to hit delete," something" told him to apply for the job. Justin chose not to contact Wade about the job. He really did not want to talk to him. He had concerns about how it would to work in Wade's family business.

Ultimately, he applied for the position. Within a couple weeks the company conducted two phone interviews, cleared his background investigation and hired him. He put his condo up for sale and put in his two-week notice to his firm. Before the month was over, his condo was sold. How often does that happen? Although Justin was hesitate to admit it he knew it was God helping him out. Who was he to argue?

In November 2011, Justin moved to Beaufort, put the majority of his belongings in storage and rented a small apartment. Because he was accustomed to big city life, his plan was to live in Charleston and work in Beaufort, until he realized how far it was. Seventy miles between the two cities… almost an hour and a half away. He did not think driving seventy miles one way twice a day was how he wanted to spend his time; time he could use to do something enjoyable… once he figured out what "enjoyable activities" meant in Beaufort. In Detroit he commuted using public transportation because it was convenient and he didn't have to worry about being arrested for drunk driving. Driving just was not his thing. Another reason to stay in Beaufort was that he remembered how beautiful the city and surrounding areas were from the times he visited, as a child, during Gullah Festival with his parents. He decided that a small, quiet town might be just what he needed.

He remembered the last time he heard from Grace she lived in South Carolina, but, at this moment in time, he did not want to see her. He was sure she would be married with twelve kids. Right now, he had to wrap his head around moving back to South Carolina, the place he swore he would never return to… ever. And even though it occurred over a year ago, he still couldn't shake his

"Saul" experience … Jesus knocking him off his horse and talking to him out loud! "Where is all of this leading to", he wondered.

"Train up a child in the way he should go; and when he is old, he will not depart from it" Proverbs 22:6 (KJV)

CHAPTER TWENTY-THREE

Meeting #13:
"The Wheels Keep Turning Round and Round"

The new department was a great success. Everyone's personality and expertise fit very well together. One of the maintenance personnel was someone that Antonio worked with while in the Navy. While visiting Lizanne in Washington DC he turned a corner and stumbled over a homeless man sitting against the wall. As he was apologizing to the man he thought he recognized him. The man immediately recognized Antonio; he even tried standing to salute him. It hurt Antonio's heart realizing this homeless man was a decorated Iraqi War veteran by the name of Josiah Johnson, one of the best large engine and diesel mechanics Antonio had ever met. Josiah could stand back, listen to the engine and know exactly what was wrong with the truck. Antonio insisted Josiah allow him to help him. Although he first resisted, Josiah finally relented. At a nearby thrift store Antonio purchased Josiah clothes and shoes. Antonio took him to his hotel to shower and change clothes and then to a nearby restaurant for lunch and to catch.

Whenever Josiah wasn't crying and when his mouth wasn't full, he told Antonio what happened to him. "Sir, when we were in the field, working our butts off for our country, we just don't think about what could happen when it's all over." He paused to take a drink. "I never thought my life would end up like this, homeless, sleeping on a park bench. After Iraq, the Navy determined that I could 'no longer do my job effectively with the injuries I sustained.' So they medically retired me and sent me out the door. I wasn't too worried because I get a retirement check and a disability check every month – on time. I knew I could still repair and drive trucks, I just could not run across a battle field carrying a back pack and weapon anymore. They made sure I had proper medical care. Since I'm from DC it made it really easy because I can go to any military hospital in the area. Also, I'm set up with Veteran's benefits so I have my own doctors and everything. I thought everything would be great for me and my family. I guess my wife did not see it that way. After the first year she decided I was too much trouble. She told me she did not want to be bogged down with an invalid." He closed his eyes and shook his head as if to shake away the look on her face. "She left me and filed for a divorce. As a part of the divorce agreement her lawyer manage to convince the judge that my injuries in Iraq caused her pain and suffering and lessened her expected quality of life. As a result, the judge gave her half of my medical retirement check, my children and my house – that I had to continue to pay the mortgage on. Thank God they could not touch my disability. They tried." Antonio asked, "What was your lawyer doing, nothing!?" Josiah said, "Basically, at least he saved my disability. He let them take my children, my house, basically, my life." The waitress interrupted them to see if they needed anything else. "I had a job working on trucks that I liked and my boss liked my work. Everything was going great until my boss retired and the new supervisor came in. I was having a few medical problems, but I made every effort not to take off for appointments as much as possible. It didn't matter because the new boss eventually found a way to get rid of me. He called it downsizing, but he really didn't like veterans, especially wounded and disabled veterans.

Supposedly he was in the military and dishonorably discharged for desertion. I overhead him talk about how wounded warriors milk the system for every penny they could get." Josiah frowned and lowered his head. "I'm sure you have other things to do, Sir, and I don't want to take up anymore of your time." Antonio looked at his watch and said, "I have plenty of time. I would like to know how you ended up here." Josiah sighed, "Okay." He paused again while the waitress came to check on them. "I had a hard time finding another job that would compensate for having to pay the mortgage on my wife's house and my apartment rent, but I did found one. Because I couldn't pay the rent and the mortgage I lost my apartment. When I lost my apartment, she went back to court and told them I was homeless and had no place to bring my children for our visitation". Josiah could feel the tears swelling up in his eyes again. He tried to stop them but he couldn't. Antonio said nothing. He just waited for Josiah to speak. "They took away my unlimited visitation with my children and made me have supervised visitation. The company I was working for shut down and I've been homeless and jobless for two years. I've only seen my kids five times in the last two years." He had to stop to wipe his face because he could feel the humiliation and the tears. "Fortunately, I did not get into drugs or trouble and I still have my benefits. I go to the doctor, when necessary, but it's hard getting into a Veteran's Home and a bed in the city shelters were never guaranteed." Antonio sat back in his chair and tried to digest it all. All he could think about was the problems he had when he and Jasmine divorced. "WOW!" is all he could say.

Antonio told Josiah about MMTrucking and the veteran's boarding house his father had created. He told him that if he ever decided to relocate to the Beaufort area there would be a job and room available for him. Two months later Josiah was hired as the lead mechanic for the government department.

Maria was very pleased with the accountant hired for the newly developed government department of MMTrucking, Justin Webster. Lizanne didn't work with the accountants or the finance portion of the contract, so she was not aware that her brother had been hired as the accountant for the contract until about a month after he was hired. They had spoken occasionally during his move, but she didn't ask him about the company he would be working for. She just remembered him saying it was a small company and he was still looking for a firm in Charleston.

It didn't take Justin long to become acclimated to the personality of MMTrucking. He, Maria and Antonio got along and interacted well. For only having one account, they kept him very busy. He was responsible for every aspect of the financial obligations of the contract, including payroll and benefits of the contract personal. He was also responsible for quarterly financial reports required for the Washington office and he made sure he didn't have to worry about the IRS or FBI sitting at his desk.

He was grateful for the slower pace of Beaufort. He even experienced the DragonBoat Race Day which is held every Labor Day Weekend. He was impressed that this little town had such a lively festival; not quite the caliber of the jazz festival in Detroit, but much better than other festivals. He did not have a date for the weekend. He had been occupied with his new job and settling down. His social life was non-existent. He was happy just learning about the city… and about himself… sober. He was enjoying this new him. He was sober, living in a small town, and only a couple hours from where he grew up. He spoke to his father, but had not yet visited him. He knew he would need to make that trip sooner than later, but he decided that this weekend was not sooner… maybe next weekend.

His high from such a great weekend crashed as soon as he walked into his office on Tuesday morning. Before he could take one sip of his coffee, who would walk into his office, uninvited, but Wade Martin. Wade was excited to find out his old friend was working with MMTrucking. Wade was not privy to any of the company's management decisions, so he was unaware of who had been hired into the new department. He was surprised to find out that Justin was the new accountant. Of course, he had ulterior motives for being in Justin's office. It wasn't because he missed his old friend.

CHAPTER TWENTY-FOUR

Meeting #14

"The Visit"

Lizanne decided to invite me on a tour of MMTrucking and the school. We met at 9:00 a.m., walking all around the facilities. It is amazing that she is part of all of this. She does not, on any level, resemble a woman co-owner of a trucking company. Now don't get me wrong, I'm not saying women must look a certain way to work in the trucking industry. I'm just saying Lizanne didn't have that industrial-like-to-get-dirty-girl look. I really think she would agree with me.

One day, Antonio and I were on a phone conference discussing specifications for a particular job order, when Antonio mentioned how pleased he was with Justin. I didn't have anything to do with accountants or finances of the contracts, so there was no conflict of interest because Justin was my brother. There was never a reason for us to talk about accountants, but he kept right on talking about Justin and how great he was.

When the meeting was over, Antonio asked me if he could come to Washington for a visit Labor Day weekend, not for work, but to see me. My brain said "no", but my mouth said yes! After I hung up the phone, I wanted to call him back and tell him "I forgot,

I will be in Istanbul that weekend and would have to take a rain check", but I didn't. Instead, I went home and started deciding what to wear. I decided to fill the weekend with every festivity available and maybe we would not get into *too* much trouble. "Ridiculous, what was I thinking!"

Shaking her head she said, "If I had just said no then, we would not be writing this book now."

Antonio and I talked about ourselves and where our past had led us. He talked a lot about his dad and mom. He truly missed his mom. His dad was not as energetic these days. We talked about my life after James. I told him, "to be honest, I was miserable after James was killed. I didn't think I would ever meet another man that could be what James was to me. I had decided the only man that truly deserved my love was dead and I had taught myself to be selfish and closed minded when it came to the needs of other people, except for my children. I contained my emotions so that when the next one died, it wouldn't really matter."

I should have just said no the first time he asked me out for dinner and that Labor Day Weekend in Washington, I definitely should have said no, but I was lonely and weak that weekend. Neither of us was ready for what happened that weekend. I warned him I was still angry. He said he could handle it. I will never forget what he said the first evening. "*I knew on Tuesday at 9:13 God might have answered my prayers and now I know God had answered my prayers. Lizanne I just need to know what you feel. Do you feel that there is any chance for us at all?*"

I wanted to say under no circumstances. I wanted to run away and forget all of this. Nevertheless, what I said was "*yes*." All he said was "*I'll see you in the morning*," got in a cab and went to his hotel. Not even a kiss. What was that all about! I was actually glad because I didn't think I could have handled any nakedness and all that …"*you know what I mean.*" We spent the rest of the weekend exploring Washington. We had a wonderful time dancing, concerts, the best food, walking and talking.

Sunday afternoon while we were walking through the monuments, I told him I had resigned from my position at the agency. He stopped walking and just looked at me. I wasn't sure if he was angry or happy. I don't think that at that moment he was either. He asked me why and I told him because I wanted to move away from the grief and heartache that plagued me day and night in this city. There was hardly a place I could go that James and I had not been there. An opportunity arose to sell our restaurant. And after talking it over with my son, who will be heading to college in January, we decided to sell. Justin and I decided to move closer to our father, who is quite elderly and suffering from mid-stage Dementia. That is one of the reasons Justin was excited to see your job announcement. Justin is already in Beaufort and I will be moving home with my dad at the end of the year. I already have my house on the market and have identified a school for Tia and Jamie.

For a moment he was quiet, as if he was processing everything. Then he asked me where in South Carolina I would be moving. I told him about 40 miles from Beaufort. The strangest look can across his face. I said, "I would have had to relinquish my position soon, even if I weren't moving, because it would have become a conflict of interest. I was about to be promoted to project manager for the department that your contract falls under. I did not want to ask Justin to resign in order for me to keep my job." Antonio nodded and then he said, "God answered my prayers."

Seeing the look on my face he explained, "Unlike you and James, when my wife and I divorced, I knew that I probably should not have married her in the first place. When we divorced I was still in the Navy and traveling and didn't have time to worry about another woman. When I retired I was extremely busy with my father and the business, as well as my son and daughter. I just didn't have time to worry about a companion. But recently, I have been realizing that I am alone and miserable as well. I asked God to send me the woman that was to be my true wife." We were walking and at that point in the conversation, I needed to sit down. He reminded me that he knew the moment he saw me at the first meeting that I was the answer to his prayers. He had reservation because we worked together and he couldn't see how that would work out. He said God told him not to worry about it. "Everything would work out as it should."

He then said to me that he knew *I would be his wife*, but I had to let him know when I knew that he would be my husband. I was glad we had sat down because I was weak. He was saying *he was ready to marry me*. I told him, again, that I wasn't ready to love anyone again. He said he would wait. I was so overwhelmed with whatever it was I was feeling I just started crying. I told him I had to go home and I would meet him at the Kennedy Center for the play. I hailed a cab and left him standing there.

CHAPTER TWENTY-FIVE

The "Godfather?" ...

"Really?" ...

When Antonio returned from his Labor Day vacation with Lizanne, he had to deal with the matter of Wade, along with Wade's debts and plans to sabotage MMTrucking. At this point, the only reason he cared at all was because he wanted to honor his father's wishes. Although, it did not include, bailing Wade out of debt and probably death every few months. If he continued bailing Wade out of trouble, Antonio and the business would be broke. Several weeks ago Antonio received an anonymous note delivered to his office by a courier that said:

"YOUR BROTHER IS MESSING WITH THE WRONG PEOPLE.

IF HE DOES NOT CLEAR HIS DEBTS, YOU WILL HAVE A DEAD BROTHER ON YOUR HANDS!"

The courier did not wait for a response and there was no name and no return address. Antonio showed the note to Maria, who just looked at him as if to ask, "What are YOU going to do about THIS!" Antonio responded as if she had actually spoken. "I don't know what I'm going to do about this." He called their lawyer. When Mr. Johnson arrived, Antonio didn't say a word; he just handed him the note. Maria thinking out loud said, "There is really no way to trace the note without hiring a forensic person to do whatever it is they do!" Mr. Johnson laughed, "A forensic scientist would conduct an analysis of the paper, fingerprints and whatever else it is they do… for $1000 an hour." "Instead, why don't you hire a private investigator to follow Wade's movements?"

So, Antonio hired a private investigator, Matt Lewis, to investigate Wade's activities and associates. Antonio and his sisters were discussing Matt Lewis's report when Wade walked into the office. The report stated that Wade owed approximately $100,000.00 in gambling and loan debt and about $10,000.00 in drug debt. Antonio stood up, "What!? I understand gambling debt, but how in the world can someone have drug dealer debt?!" Maria suggested sending him to their cousin in Mexico. Although Antonio and Esabelle wanted to agree, they both said "no". Antonio, Maria and Isabelle were discussing what they were going do about the debt and Wade when he walked into Antonio's office. Wade was unaware they knew about the debt and Wade did not know about the threat on his life. When Wade said he needed Antonio to give him the money, Antonio knew it was time to cut him off. It was time for an intervention. They were all getting too old for this nonsense. Damned if they do, damned if they don't. If they continued giving him money, he will never stop. If they did not help Wade at some point they would be burying him.

Matt Lewis had more disturbing news about underhanded events that were about to happen involving Wade. Wade knew he was in bigger trouble than he could talk himself out of. He had little to sell or use as collateral because he spent most of his money on drugs and gambling. He had to get money from somewhere quick! He was familiar with drug trafficking; after all he trafficked drugs right under his father's nose for months before the idiot driver got caught. Wade and the 'voices' laughed when he thought about

Chris. He was just plain stupid and deserved what he got.

However, it was not funny when he remembered he was attacked and had almost been beaten to death when the drugs were confiscated. He did not have the money or drugs to return to the drug dealer. He was lucky someone called the police, otherwise he would have died that night. He felt lucky today, years later, that the only repercussion of that dreadful event was a very noticeable limp on the left side of his body and the "voices" had grown louder.

While Wade was in the hospital after the attack, Esabelle was on shift and came to visit him. When she opened the door, she heard him talking out loud to someone. When she came into the room there was no one, only Wade. His facial expression was quite distorted. When she asked him who he was talking to, he said "them" and pointed in the direction of the TV. However the TV wasn't on. She mentioned the episode to his doctor who, of course, knew Wade was schizophrenic. Unfortunately, because of Wade's request that his illness not be disclosed, the doctor did not reveal any information to the family. His doctor made sure he received his medication. The next day Esabelle mentioned the incident to Wade but he didn't remember it. Esabelle told him he was blessed the night he was attacked. He wanted to correct her by saying that his recovery had nothing to do with blessings, divine intervention or God, but he didn't; however, his response was "anything he does, anything he gets, anything that happens or doesn't happen for him, is not about God; it's all his own doing." Later that day, Esabelle made a point to mention the incident to Antonio and Maria.

On Labor Day Wade was sitting in a restaurant eating breakfast when, without invitation, a gentleman just took it upon himself to sit at his table. He was immediately furious until he looked up at the man and realized it was Christopher Gregory who had been released from prison a couple months ago. Christopher did not waste time with nice conversation, "Mr. Wade Martin. How's life been treating you?" "I saw you walk in, why are you walking with a limp," he sneered? "I heard you had a little *accident*" he said very sarcastically. Chris continued, "I did not appreciate being setup and thrown under the bus just so you could save your own skin. I heard your daddy sent you off to rehab. I wonder if that was to get you off drugs or to get you out of the way for a while. I'm sure he needed a break from you," he laughed. Wade glared at Chris but he didn't say anything. Chris continued. "You know, it's ironic that, even while in jail, I maintained my business and you, Mr. Martin, couldn't hold down a job; even your little brother fired you." "You wanna know what else is ironic, you have a $10,000 drug debt and a $100,000 gambling loan debt and no clue as to how you will pay it back." Wade sat up in his chair as Chris leaned back in his. Chris had a very ominous smile as he watched the smirk on Wade's face fade as he was becoming visibly distressed. When Wade regained his composure he asked Chris, "How do you know *who* I owe *what* to." He took a breath because 'the voices' were screaming and telling him "just hit him in the face! " Wade said in as calm a voice as he could muster, "And why is any of my business your concern, Mr. Gregory?" Wade was struggling to keep his voice low, but he was livid and the 'voices' were screaming. Wade scoffed, "Why are you still disturbing my breakfast?" Chris leaned close, placing on the table not only the IOUs Wade signed for drugs but also the IOUs he signed for the gambling loan debts. He laid those papers down so smooth you'd have thought he had a hand full of spades and was about to clean the table. Chris leaned a little closer with his fingers stroking his nicely low cut beard, and said, "What you didn't know, Mr. Martin, is that you were buying drugs from me." Squinting just a little Chris continued, "I made it possible for you to get all the drugs you wanted. I bought your gambling loan from my good friend, Mario. I told him not to get his hands dirty trying to squeeze blood out of a turnip. I told him I know just how to handle you, don't I Mr. Martin." Chris set there for a moment and watched Wade squirm a little more. "You see, Mario's plan was to hurt your family, but you and I both know that you could care less about your family, isn't that right?"

Chris explained how he ran a successful drug and other commodities import and export business from prison. He was the self-proclaimed "Godfather" of Beaufort. "I watched as you dug yourself deeper and deeper into a hole, robbing Peter to pay Paul." "I knew you were a junkie and a gambler." "I knew you threw me under the bus to take the rap for the drug bust, and I know that you thought you'd seen the last of Christopher Gregory." Again, Chris sat back in his chair." After a moment Chris pulled his chair close to the table. "Remember your "little" incident in the alley those years ago. It should have been a warning to you. I see it wasn't. You think you are smart and can handle your mess." "I made sure you bought drugs from my dealers. I allowed you to get deeper and deeper into debt until I had you right where I wanted you." Chris looked around the room then looked at Wade, shaking his head, "the reason you are so pitiful is because you never understood that there were smarter wolves in the pack than you."

"I'll be in touch after the holiday. I have a proposition, Wade, that I think you will not dare refuse." Wade said nothing. Chris stood and held out his hand to shake because there is honor, even among thieves. Wade wasn't feeling honorable. Chris laughed and walked out of the restaurant.

Wade was dumbfounded. He did not know what to do or think. How did he get himself in this mess? He was about to call on the name of the Lord when that evil voice reminded him of how much he disliked God, and this was proof of how God could care less about him. He said to himself, actually out loud, "who did that little punk street-rat think he was.' Then he took a deep breath and sank into his chair as he remembered that little street-rat had the IOUs and his life in his pocket.

Now, Wade was indebted $110,000 or more to the man he framed. Wade knew that his insane hatred and his "voices" had backfired on him. He was about to lose everything. The "voices' laughed. That was the first time he wondered if the 'voices' were really on his side.

Matt Lewis was glad he decided to plant a bug on Wade because there would be no way he would remember all of this. He also "procured" some information about other ventures Mr. Gregory was involved in that might come in handy later.

Wade knew his only recourse was to go to Antonio, again. He hated the idea of telling him what transpired. He then remembered that his good friend, Justin Webster, not only lived nearby, but he was an accountant at MMTrucking. Wade thought he just might be able to kill two birds with one stone. He would approach Justin, test the water, see where his head is, and then hit him up for a loan. He thought, "How do you ask someone you haven't seen in 30 years for a loan for $110,000?" Well, desperate times call for desperate measures. He also hoped that Justin had not lost his "bad" side; maybe they could conspire something together that would make him and get Chris off of his back. Unfortunately, before he could even pose his proposition to Justin, Antonio interrupted. And of course it did not go well when Wade told Antonio about the debt. Wade didn't know Antonio already knew about the contact between him and Chris.

CHAPTER TWENTY-SIX
"There's a Snake in the Hen House"

*"Now the serpent was more crafty than any of the wild animals the Lord
God had made…"*
(Genesis 3:1a NIV)

When hired, Justin made it known that he knew Wade from
his childhood, but that he had not had contact with him in over 30
years. Antonio and Maria decided to tell him of the difficulties the
company suffered over the years because of Wade. They also
informed Justin that they had no intention of bringing him back into
the company in any capacity after his last episode. They told him
how disgruntled and extremely unpredictable Wade had become.
There was no reason for Wade to come in the office or school
buildings. If Wade stepped foot on the premises, they were to be
notified immediately. They especially wanted to keep him away
from the other drivers. Maria made sure Justin understood the
quickest way to lose his job was to start affiliating with Wade in any
manner. After the fiasco with his company in Detroit Justin was not
taking any chances, so when Wade showed up in his office he
immediately emailed Maria and Antonio to let them know. As soon
as he hit send, Wade's cell phone rang and he excused himself. He
then came back to say something had come up and he would have
to finish their visit another day. That was when he knew, without a
doubt, Wade had something up his sleeve and that he would have
to watch his back. He created a folder on his computer labeled
"CYA." In it he created a sub-folder named "Wade Martin" and he
saved the email there, just in case. Again, he was grateful for the

CYA class he took in college. It had come in handy more than once and he thought it would come in handy again.

Wade was furious Antonio found out so quickly that he was in the building. Who tipped him and what gave that "half-and-half" the right to have spies watching out for when he came around. He wanted to storm into his office. Regrettably, he couldn't; he needed to be nice to his little brother. He hated him, however, he needed him right now, so he had to be civil.

When he arrived at Antonio's office the secretary told him he was in a meeting. He didn't care. Despite her protest, he just walked into Antonio's office. To his surprise, there was his siblings, Antonio, Maria and Esabelle. Wade wanted to know why he wasn't invited to the meeting, but he knew he wasn't consulted on business matters. They might even be discussing him, he just didn't know to what extent. He was right, they were discussing him. After niceties, Maria and Esabelle excused themselves leaving Antonio and Wade in the office… to talk.

Wade decided not to ask them what they were talking about. He said, "I need a little advance on my stipend because I need to settle some "debts" immediately." Again, Antonio asked "Wade what happens to your money from month to month? You should never be broke." Wade immediately got an attitude. He exclaimed quite loudly, "I don't need anyone keeping up with me or my money. I came to ask a favor, to see if my brother could help me out. If not, just say so!" Antonio didn't respond and Wade remembered he was begging. "I'm sorry man, I'm just a little on edge" he said as he calmed down. "I ran into someone from my past that I would have just as soon never saw again," Antonio asked, "Wade does this debt have anything to do with drugs or gambling and when do you need it by." Wade didn't want to answer either of those questions. After he didn't answer Antonio said, "I just got back in town and I have a meeting shortly that I have to prepare for." Wade headed for the door. Antonio said, "Wade if you couldn't be straight about why you need the money, I will not help you." Wade stormed out of the office mumbling curse words under his breath.

CHAPTER TWENTY-SEVEN

"Fires... Fires..."

When Antonio returned home, he didn't have time to ponder the weekend events with Lizanne. He had to deal with the matter of Wade, his debts and a rival company called McIntosh Trucking.

He sat at his desk, looking at the documents in front of him. He wondered why his dad was placing such a burden on him... to take care of Wade. Wade was the oldest, yet he was responsible for him. Why? Antonio remembered Isabelle talking about her visit with Wade in the hospital and him talking to "no one" out loud. He wondered if his dad knew that there might be something wrong with Wade. And if so, why didn't he tell him about it. Antonio felt as if he was fighting invisible demons on a daily basis when it came to Wade. It just shouldn't be this hard.

Nevertheless, he continued to care for Wade because he was his brother and because he wanted to honor his father's wishes. Antonio remembered how much he loved his big brother and how he wanted to be around him all the time. He also remembered how he ignored the way Wade treated him, like a step-brother, like a half-and-half. He just prayed that taking care of Wade would not cause the downfall of MMTrucking. If he continued on this path, Antonio and the business would be broke.

Matt Lewis was reporting to him almost every day concerning Wade's movements. When Wade told Antonio he needed a larger amount of money Antonio knew that even at his age, Wade was still a liar, a cheat and the truth was not in him, not even a little bit. He knew that Wade would continue using the family and the family business to bail him out of his mess.

Wade had several disturbing plans in the fire, all of which had the potential to harm MMTrucking. He secretly started buying stock in MMTrucking, which is not illegal and under normal circumstances would not be a problem; except that normal business owners do not buy their own stock.

Matt Lewis overheard a conversation between McIntosh and Wade about sabotaging the company. Wade would help McIntosh steal some of MMTrucking's contractors and under bid upcoming contracts. Matt Lewis advised Antonio that Wade needed to be watched carefully.

Wade had several meetings with Joseph McIntosh, owner of McIntosh Trucking out of Charleston. McIntosh was shrewd and borderline dishonest in his business endeavors. It was rumored he transported more than contractual materials. He bought out a couple smaller companies, promising to retain the drivers and at their current salary. He reneged on that promise before the ink was dry on the contract. Several of the drivers were now driving for MMTrucking. He had submitted a proposal for the same government contract that MMTrucking was awarded. It was rumored he lost the bid because of his reputation in the industry. McIntosh wanted to buy out MMTrucking when Marcus retired. He thought Antonio was green and would not be able to maintain the business. Of course Wade was all for the sale, which would have killed two birds with one stone for him. He would have immediate cash available and Antonio would not be in control of anything. When McIntosh didn't even get an invitation to discuss it, he told

Antonio the next time he saw him, MMTrucking would be bankrupt. Wade and McIntosh saw an ally in each other to be used at a later date. That day was today.

Wade met with McIntosh to discuss the possibility of a merger between MMTrucking and McIntosh Trucking. Wade didn't even have any negotiating power to decide what brand of toilet paper they would use, but he decided he would meet with McIntosh and "talk" about possibilities. The talks were of interest to McIntosh because MMTrucking had assets that he did not have. He also didn't like the idea of this small town company out-bidding him on several major contracts.

Wade knew his best chance of getting out from under Chris Gregory was to offer him something that would be of interest to him, drivers and trucks. He knew of three or four drivers who were squeaky clean on paper, but had "side businesses" that would be lucrative for both Wade and Chris. It would be easy to get to the drivers and proposition them, except for the one who drives for the government contract. He had to get to Justin for that driver.

Chris was very confident in his hold on Wade, so when they met, he laid out the plan for Wade's "restitution." Chris wanted a lump sum that he felt was reasonable in the amount of $50,000 plus $5,000 per month until he decided it was enough. If Wade did not agree to these terms, he would contact his family and the newspaper to tell his story. This threat was a little disturbing, but Wade would just bid his time. While Chris was rattling off his demands, Wade was strategizing his next moves. If he played his cards right, he would get rid of the debt, Chris Gregory and MMTrucking all at the same time. The only person that could ruin his plans was Antonio Martin. Wade thought, it's too bad he couldn't get rid of him too… and then again, maybe he can. His attention was jolted back to Chris when he heard him say that the deadline to start paying the $50,000 was next Friday and every day after the deadline would cost him $1,000.00 until he pays up or until he's dead… whichever came first. Wade sneered as he told Chris that threats would get him nowhere. He had something that was worth more than any amount of money he owed him, or his life.

Mr. Antonio Luis Martin

and

Ms. Lizanne W. McKenzie

Cordially invite you to celebrate the union of their families

In Holy Matrimony

On December 2, 2012

"Let him kiss me with the kisses of his mouth: for thy love is better than wine."

Song of Solomon 1:2

CHAPTER TWENTY-EIGHT

Meeting #15:

"Observations"

Lizanne asked me to meet her at the hospital where Antonio had been admitted for "observation." "That's what they say when they are not sure what's going on." We met in the cafeteria and she handed me an invitation for their wedding.

I didn't give him an answer to his proposal right away. It was about a week before I called him. He was really busy and somewhat agitated over matters with the business, so I just told him to call me when he could talk. When he called I told him, "I had analyzed and agonized over his proposal. I prayed and prayed and talked to my children. I kept saying I was not wife material at that point; I didn't want to make myself vulnerable to anyone except my children. Everyone important in my life has died or almost died." "My father is dying which is why I am moving closer to him. I'm so tired of caring for sick people. If I become a wife, I'd have to share myself, my energy with my husband. I'd have to be there through thick and thin and I can't do that. Actually, I don't want to do that." He didn't say a word for what seemed like a day and a half. He then said he would call me back later and he hung up the phone. I thought, "Great! That's over! Now, I can get back to being miserable alone."

Not so! He called me back about two days later and said that his mother taught him about the power of fasting and praying. *"Every time he would say something about God and his faith it threw me off because I wanted him to be a heathen. That would be one more reason not to marry him!"* Anyway, he said he needed to consult with 'his' God, as if his God was different from my God. *Maybe that was what he thought that I was a heathen because I was so selfish."* He said his God told him I was his "Ruth." He said, "It didn't matter to him what I had gone through, what I thought I could, or even wanted to do. It didn't matter if I didn't believe that "my God" could wipe away pain. He knew that his God will. He said God told him he would have his true wife and no matter what I was thinking, everything would be fine in the end. I was like, WHAT! I tried to explain to him again, but this time, he cut me off and said if it was ok with me he would like to get married sooner than later. So, I said okay and we were married on December 2, 2012. And you know what, I was happy and excited and terrified.

We had a small but elegant wedding in South Carolina with our families. Justin brought our father to the wedding. He was unable to officiate or walk me down the aisle, however, he was able to read a scripture and say the prayer. That made him very happy. I was honored to have Marcus walk me down the aisle. He was so happy that Antonio was happy. The only problem we had with Marcus was that he insisted on wearing his uniform, which he kept cleaned in his closet "just in case." We all prayed that it didn't fit… Praise God He STILL answers prayers.

We honeymooned in the mountains in North Carolina. Both of us had been overseas and to the "islands" so the mountains were a pleasant change of scenery.

Before we were married, Antonio told me about his family, about MMTrucking and his brother Wade. Almost as an afterthought I said, "Wait a minute, *Wade Martin* is your brother?" He said, "*Yes, do you know him?*" I said, "*Yes, he went to my high school and tutored my brother for a while.*" He knew that Wade was very smart, but he couldn't believe that he would tutor anyone. I told him "your brother was bad news and I always wondered if something was not quite right with him, no offense." Antonio said "none taken." I told him some of the things he did, as well as the type of people he hung out with in school, which made no sense because he was very, very smart. Wade actually tutored kids in math, my brother Justin being one of them. Wade was so angry at his family and God. It was very scary, to the point that I advised my dad several times to sever the relationship with my brother and Wade. Wade had influenced my brother to blame God for my mother's death. As a result, Justin has struggled spiritually for a long time. "Wow, Wade Martin will be my brother-in-law... that's terrible" I smirked. Antonio rolled his eyes and said "for better or for Wade!"

Antonio told me Wade was trying to sabotage the business and it was becoming a big problem. He suspected that Wade had a mental illness, but he has no proof. Antonio said Justin told them he was acquainted with Wade from his childhood, but he didn't go into details. Wade did approach Justin, but Justin didn't talk with him, at least not so far.

I spoke to Justin I asked him about Wade. He told me the same thing. He could sense Wade had a reason for seeking him out and it had nothing to do with catching up on old times. I reminded him of how far he had come and to watch his back and his salvation. Of course he reminded me that he was for real grown, but that he would be sure to let me know if he needed me.

CHAPTER TWENTY-NINE

"Birds of a feather..."

It's interesting how people with no scruples seek out people with no scruples...

Wade met with Christopher Gregory offering him a "partnership" along with him and McIntosh. They would use the trucks to transport various types of goods. This greatly interested Chris as he wanted to expand his territory, and he needed transport to do that.

Wade and McIntosh devised a plan that, if successful, would derail MMTrucking. He "acquired" a list of the contracts held by MMTrucking as well as upcoming bids. Sheila, a new employee, was not informed of Wade's history with the company, so when he asked her for copies of the files, she gave them to him. McIntosh used the list to lure two companies away from Antonio by offering them "incentives." Several of the companies McIntosh approached were not interested in negotiating a new contract with him. One of the chief executive officer contacted Antonio asking why another company was trying to buy them out.

The 'voices' were beginning to talk more and sometimes they convinced Wade to do irrational things that backfired. He decided to help some of the other companies make the decision to move. He emailed, from his personal email account, the local paper with an "anonymous tip" that MMTrucking was in financial trouble. It was rumored Antonio Martin, Chief Executive Officer of MMTrucking, was embezzling money from the company and the company would be negotiating a bankruptcy settlement.

What Wade did not realize was that the paper would not run the story without verification. Neither he nor McIntosh remembered that God uses the deeds of the unrighteous to benefit the righteous.

The journalist contacted MMTrucking's attorney, Mr. Johnson, to verify the story. Of course Mr. Johnson didn't know what the reporter was talking about. Mr. Johnson called for an emergency meeting with Antonio and Matt Lewis. When he heard what was going on, Antonio went into damage control mode, military style. They sent a private email to all of the contract chief executive officers, including the ones that left, informing them they were not selling their contracts, nor were they planning to walk away from any of their contracts.

The next day, they called an emergency meeting with the company board of directors to let them know that someone was attempting to sabotage the company by planting false information with the local paper. After that meeting, Matt Lewis contacted a friend of his at the sheriff's office.

"Some become fools through their rebellious ways and suffered affliction because of their iniquities" (Psalms 107:17 NIV)

Wade waited for the explosion. It didn't happen. What did happen was Wade was arrested for allegedly sending false accusations to the newspaper, allegedly falsifying company documents and forgery. This time he went to jail for himself. There was no one to frame. Wade implicated Joseph McIntosh and Christopher Gregory. Both squealed like little piglets and testified against Wade. Wade begged Antonio to bail him out. When Antonio didn't, Wade cursed him. He called him all kinds of horrible names that I won't repeat.

When Wade was arrested, he was unable to take his medication. His family did not know he was on medication for a mental illness. His doctor had no privileges at the jail. By the time he found out that Wade had been arrested Wade had had a psychotic episode. His family was very upset to find out Wade had been diagnosed for years with schizophrenia and bi-polar disorder, that he refused to tell them or allow his doctor to disclose. However, it explains many bizarre behaviors that he explained away and the two times he overdosed because he was taking both legal and illegal drugs.

Although he was receiving medication again, while in court the 'voices' were loud making him speak out of turn on a couple occasions. Antonio asked the bailiff permission for he or one of his sisters to sit closer to Wade, hoping that might calm him down.

Wade was found guilty and sentenced to a three year jail term. Because he was diagnosed with these mental illnesses, the courts ordered him to serve a two year sentence in a psychiatric hospital instead of the county jail. The final years was dismissed as time served while awaiting trail and during trial. He could have been sentenced for a longer term but under the circumstances the court chose to be lenient. He received a very good deal. Despite his arrogance toward God, God allowed the South Carolina Justice System to show him grace. It was sad. He was close to sixty years old. If he didn't pull himself together while incarcerated, he could die before he gets out. Chris Gregory could not take him to court to recoup his money and risk going to jail again for drug trafficking, so he lost out. Joseph McIntosh lost any chance of acquiring MMTrucking.

And all was well with the world for MMTrucking, but not for Antonio

Antonio was heartbroken his brother had gone to such lengths to destroy him for something that happened before he was born. He worried about what would happen to him in prison. He wondered if his brother would ever find peace with himself and with God. He decided he would visit him as often as possible, even if Wade didn't want to see him. Maybe he might be able to find a clear spot in his spirit that will hear him and hear God. One of the psychiatrists in the hospital was a member of Lizanne's church. He visited Wade whenever he could. However, Wade had completely shut down. He tried blaming God, but he could no longer do that. He knew it was his own fault he was in this predicament.

Wade stayed to himself in the hospital. He did not associate with anyone he didn't have to, refusing to participate in any programs not required. Antonio visited him every week, sometimes Wade would see him, sometimes he wouldn't. One visit was very traumatic. The 'voices' were very loud while Antonio tried to talk to him about making changes and reading the bible. Wade yelled, cursed him, told him he never liked him and called him a half-and-half. Antonio sat there allowing him to rant at him for a few minutes. Then he left.

CHAPTER THIRTY

"Safe in His Arms"

In the mist of Wade's sabotage attempt, there was another battle going on having nothing to do with MMTrucking. When Lizanne moved to Beaufort, one of her goals was to quickly find a church. Even though she had become a professional "pew warmer" she still felt the need to stay somewhat connected in her faith. JR, Lia, Jamie and Lizanne visited several churches and finally decided on one with enough activities for Jamie and a church school. JR was in college. He was not going to be living at home, but Lizanne still wanted his opinion and he liked the church. So they started attending the next week or so.

Lia and Jamie loved the church and school. It didn't take Jamie long to find activities that interest her in both church and school. She reminded me of Justin when he was young. She was in the drama club at school and on the praise dance team at church. And she loved her fourth grade teacher, Ms. Kelly. Ms. Kelly was also the drama club teacher at school, children's Sabbath School and praise dance teacher at church. All Jamie talked about was Ms. Kelly; and how sweet and pretty she was and how she was a great dancer. One day when she was telling her Uncle Justin about school, she said the one thing she loved the most about Ms Kelly was her hair. She had beautiful hair that was long and twisted. He wondered... "Really? I knew a young lady in college named Ms.

Kelly and she had beautiful locks." "Silently he thought "Lizanne has been bugging me about going to church with her, so curiosity just gave me a reason to go."

Justin was still fighting his demons, meaning he still doubted God was available for him. He always believed that God existed, but he had several terrible experiences and was not willing to blame them on himself. He'd rather blame it on God. He enjoyed church services. Although whenever he attended, he was one of those people that came in just in time for the sermon and slipped out before the appeal. He attended church with his dad, assisting him, and sneering at the hypocrites that were still alive. He loved that he had to pull his silver Mercedes Benz SL500c convertible to the front so that his father did not have to walk from the lot. There were always one or two hypocrites at the front entrance, trying to figure out how he could afford such a car; he must be selling drugs. He would smile and give the traditional greeting "Happy Sabbath Sister or Brother so-n-so." Even his dad had to smile watching the reactions on all their faces. Even in his dementia, his dad was overjoyed that Justin comes a couple Sabbaths a month to take him to church. Justin did not attend church when he stayed in Beaufort. He just wasn't in the frame of mind to dedicate himself to any church. Now, because of Jamie, Grace was on his mind more and more. He wondered if she was his niece's teacher. The true reason he delayed searching her out was because he didn't think she was ready to see him. The last time they spoke, she was clear, he had to evict his demons and embrace God the Father, God the Son and God the Holy Spirit. He finally conquered two demons, marijuana and alcohol. He attended his AA meetings regularly and stayed sober by occupying his mind with other, healthier, activities. He became involved with the lives of his niece and nephew. He provides free tax services at the community center near his house during tax season and he teaches accounting at the local technical college. He was working on it, but he was still an emotional and spiritual mess.

The closer it came to the weekend, the more anxiety Justin felt. He did not have to go to his dad's this weekend. Lizanne, Antonio and the girls would be visiting him for the weekend. He looked for excuses why he should not go to church. Any excuse would do but there was none. He happened to turn his radio on and thought he would be listening to jazz, but he had changed the station the night before and forgot to put it back. The voice on the radio was telling the story of Naaman the Leper.

"Naaman was a very important man in his country. His only problem was he had leprosy. He was told a prophet named Elisha could heal him. He went to see Elisha who told him to dip himself seven times into the Jordan River. Now the Jordan River was filthy dirty and he didn't want to do it. But one of his servants encouraged him to at least try it. So he dipped once - nothing; three times – nothing; five times – nothing; six times – nothing. But on the SEVENTH TIME! – HALLELUJAH!, the voice shouted. When Naaman came up the seventh time, his skin was restored and the leprosy was gone. Naaman, who had no knowledge of the true God came out of the water saying "Now I know that there is no God in all the world except in Israel..." (2Kings 5 NIV)"

The same voice he heard as a child and in his room at the rehabilitation center said to him "You knew me well and I hope you want to know me again." Justin knew he would have no peace until he accepted Christ into his life again. And at that moment he did.

He went to Lizanne's church for divine service, even though she wasn't there. He sat in the back, as was his custom, so that he could sneak out before the appeal. The music was good and the children's story was entertaining. He put 20 dollars in the offering plate. Right before the sermon a song began to play. He had never heard the song before, which wasn't surprising since he made it a point not to listen to Christian music. What caught his attention was that this song was not sung by the choir, it was piped over the intercom. And from the door next to him a praise dancer came down the aisle swaying, turning and praising along with the music, "Safe in His Arms." He was mesmerized by the music, the words of the song and her graceful movements. As he watched her movements he had a sense that there was something familiar about her. His heart began to beat just a little bit faster. He closed his eyes so that he could concentrate on the words of the song...

"When the storms of life are raging, and the billows roll ...

Yes I'm so glad that He shall hide me, Safe in His arms."

Right before the song ended he began to focus on the dancer again. She lifted her face upward in a familiar motion and he saw her... Grace. As with his first encounter with her, he wanted to run, but he didn't. He was spell bound. When the music ended, she moved swiftly to a side door and disappeared. Someone tapped him on the shoulder. The usher was handing him some tissue. He didn't even notice the tears rolling down his face. He needed to leave now! As he stepped into the foyer, there she stood, helping someone with something. He just stood there. Eventually she looked up and saw him. She ran to him and hugged his neck. Under her breath he could hear her saying, "you're here thank you God, thank you." He held her and he could feel the tears on his face. He knew then he never wanted to let her go again. Sadness came over him, even while he was holding her. He was sure she was married with children. At that thought he loosened his grip on her and smiled down at her. She was just as beautiful now as she was in college. He was having a hard time breathing, just like in college. The few people in the hall stopped what they were doing to see what was going on. She did quick introductions, "everybody this is Justin Webster. Justin this is everybody. Justin and I went to college together and I haven't seen him in 15 or 20 years." One woman came up to him, paced around him, kind of looked him up and down, and said, "*So you* are Justin Webster.*" Grace shooed her away. He smiled, remembering in college how he wanted to fall into her eyes and never come out. He asked her what was that all about? "Nosey bodies" she said. He asked her if she would be able to get away from the church to talk. He immediately retracted and said, "I'm sorry to be so crud, I didn't mean to disrespect your husband. I would just like to catch up on old times." He told her that his niece, Jamie, was in her classes, although he didn't know that her Ms. Kelly was his Grace. At that moment he noticed that she was just standing there looking up at him, smiling. He realized that he had not stopped talking. So he shut-up. Grace told him how much she loved Jamie. "She is so smart and so in love with Jesus. It is amazing that a child so young can have such insight. She did on occasion make me think about you." She then said, "Thank you for respecting me enough to respect my husband," she paused for a moment, "I would love to leave and have dinner with you. I would be traveling alone, considering I never married, and therefore, there is no husband and I am not in a relationship!" If it were biologically possible, his heart would have back flipped a couple times. They settled on a time and date then she left to tend to others, but not before she hugged him again and kissed him on the cheek. He couldn't move from that spot for a few seconds because he was melting. He knew if he moved, he would fall to the floor. His mind could only come up with three words... "THANK YOU GOD!" "Where would I be if not for Your Grace?"

They met at one of her favorite restaurants, "Sgt White's Restaurant" on Boundary Street. Plain old home cooked food. For the first few moments they just stared at each other, both wondering what to say, what to do. She wanted to touch him, but she dared not be so bold. He wanted to just look at her, until he pulled himself together. Right now, if not for his skin, he would be all over the place. They were distracted by the server, who spoke to Grace with familiarity asking what they would like to drink. Before Grace could say anything Justin asked what did they have. "Sweet Tea and water" was her response. He asked if that was it and she said yes. So he said "well in that case I'll have Sweet Tea and water, please ma'am." Grace ordered the same. They asked each other how the other was doing, then Justin told her about parts of his life since she graduated, not everything all at once. She talked about her life after college. The dinner came and soon the night was over. She had an early morning and so did he so they said their goodbyes and left the restaurant. He was upset that he didn't tell her how he felt and about his fear that she might have been married or not want him because he was still avoiding the appeal. She was upset with herself because she wanted to tell him how angry she was with him that, for so long, he choose not to love God or her. Even though she understood that he had to find his own way, she was still angry that they missed all of these years.

They did not miss any more years. They dated for about six months before he asked her to marry him. He praised God every day for being merciful and patient towards him. He praised God for showing him grace and giving him Grace.

"Your grace and mercy brought me through;

I'm living this moment because of You;

I'd like to thank You, and praise You too;

AUDREYANN C. MOSES

Your grace and mercy brought me through.

(Franklin D. Williams)

CHAPTER THIRTY-ONE
Meeting #16
"Words Are Everything"

When Antonio was diagnosed, he remembered what Lizanne said and chose not to tell her until he had no choice. If he could recover or die, he would never have to tell her.

"...Don't be afraid; you are worth more than many sparrows."
Luke 12:6b

Lizanne sat quietly for a moment staring into her cup of steaming Earl Grey tea. She looked at me with crimped lips and sad eyes. "Things had become weird between Antonio and me... mainly because of me. Our life was interrupted by Wade on so many levels and so many occasions, especially when he tried to sabotage the company. I was just through. I knew from childhood that Wade was bad news, but his actions were more than I had imagined."

"Not too long ago Antonio told me about a conversation he had with Justin and Hussein, his brother-in-law's."

In the mist of everything going on with Wade, Antonio went to Justin's office asking if he could speak to him about a private matter, maybe they could meet Hussein for lunch. He wanted to talk with both of his brother-in-law's at the same time. At first Justin thought Antonio and I were already having marital problems. Justin told me later he thought I was having emotional problems because the drunk driver who killed my first husband, James, had been released from prison with full driving privileges. Although the driver lives in Michigan, Justin felt I was having much anxiety over this set of circumstances. He was right, but as it turned out, that's not what Antonio wanted to talk to them about.

Over lunch, Antonio told them about the cancer along with the added danger to his health due to his blood pressure and diabetes. Antonio told them, "I decided to get two other medical opinions but results were the same. Early stage prostate cancer. I will need surgery and radiation. After surgery, the treatment would include a type of radioactive seeds implanted into my prostate so that I wouldn't have to go for radiation every couple days. This way, once my doctor released me, I could return to work." Hussein and Justin wasn't eating. They sat silently and listened as Antonio continued. He told them he did not know how much assistance would be necessary before or after the surgery, but hoped he would be able to depend on them. They both exclaimed, "Of course we will do whatever is necessary." He told them he was sorry to drop such a bombshell on them but there is one more thing he needed to ask them, "Please do not to tell anyone, especially not the sisters and especially not Lizanne."

I could see that Lizanne was already beginning to tear up and I had a feeling this was the easy part of the story.

Justin asked why he didn't want the sisters to know. Antonio told him, "One reason is because all of them had experienced death by cancer in their lives and he wanted to spare them as much as possible." *Lizanne looked at me with tears in her eyes.* "The other reason was because of me. Before we were married I was adamant in telling him that I was not taking care of sick, lame or crippled people, including myself. When Antonio told me about this conversation he said that Justin was instantly angry with me. But before he could go on a rampage Antonio told them that he didn't want to burden me with his illness, so he would tell me when he had no other choice and he would give me the option to bow out of the marriage if I wanted. But he would not obligate me to take care of him. He had already made arrangements for an in-home nurse to care for him for as long as possible in a separate room in the house; or go into a rehabilitation nursing home if necessary.

Hussein knew how I felt, which was why he wasn't very fond of me, but Justin was clearly disturbed. Justin told me he told Antonio "as much as she had harassed me about getting my life together and my priorities straight, she has not overcome the demons she lives with."

Both men promised not to say anything to the women… "for now."

CHAPTER THIRTY-TWO
"Oh God, Please Don't"

To tell you the truth, I had not really spoken to Antonio except for "hellos" and "goodbyes". Between the frustration of Maria and I seeing him in The Restaurant with *"that woman"* and then Wade's trial, I just did not have much to say. I still had reservations as to whether Antonio was having an affair or not. Nevertheless, Antonio asked me to loan him the money for Wade's attorney, and I did. Even though we were all angry with Wade, we didn't want a court appointed attorney causing him to spend the rest of his life in an insane asylum. Nevertheless, I was still angry at Antonio for involving me in his family mess. And I was mad at myself for marrying into this dysfunctional mess. I had enough dysfunction of my own to deal with. I just didn't have any words for him. We talked about household, company and children business. We had five children, three of which were in college. So we had to make sure funds were available to go wherever they were needed. Other than that, I really had nothing to say and he never asked me why. I guess he too was in his own world.

This particular day I had some things to discuss with him, especially about the money I paid for Wade's lawyer. I never liked Wade, but my husband asked me to help so I helped. He would not use company funds for such a private matter. He didn't want the company connected in any way to Wade, especially with the "accusations" still popping up in the news. I understood and didn't blame him for wanting to keep the company out of it. We had just paid the college tuition and fees which didn't leave much liquid personal money to spare, except for the savings from selling the restaurant. He thought about forcing Wade to sell his shares, but there still would not have been enough. So he came to me to ask if I would pay the lawyer's fee and he would reimburse me. My first thought was to slap him in the face and say "how dare you ask me... why don't you go and ask your "blank! blank!" mistress for the money!" But then I would have had to talk about how I saw him and *that woman* a few weeks ago. I didn't want to go through that. So I agreed to help, using part of the money saved from the sale of the restaurant.

I wanted to discuss with him when the money would be reimbursed and about holiday plans. Even though I was having issues with my selfish feelings towards him, we were still a great family and we were planning a trip to Germany for Christmas.

I wanted to ask about the woman, but you know what, I kept trying to convince myself that I didn't really care, as long as it didn't interfere with me, the children or our household. He could do whatever he wanted. I didn't have to worry about being all lovey-dovey with him. I had lost it for him, and actually, I don't think I ever had it. Oh, don't get me wrong, I loved him. I thought it was the best step to take in marrying him. I didn't need his business or his money. Actually, I was much more financially secure than him. I guess having a brother as an accountant helped. But there were days when I wondered why I married him. How unfair it was for him that he married a woman he wanted a whole marriage with and I didn't want the same thing with him. It's sad when I think about it. I know I was selfish.

I called Antonio's cellphone for an hour with no answer. By

the time I got home, I was upset because all I could think about was *that woman* in the restaurant and questioning why was I jealous about it. When I walked in the door, Antonio was on the floor, barely conscious.

"Oh my God!" "Oh my God!" "Antonio!" "Antonio!"

"Oh my God!" I thought he was dying. He was barely breathing... I had dropped my phone in the bottom of my purse and couldn't find it.

"Where's my phone!"

I found his phone on the floor next to him.

"Here's his phone"

When I picked up his phone to dial 911, I could see my phone number..."He was trying to call me?"

9-1-1...

"Antonio!" "Oh my God!" "Antonio! Please wake-up... please say something!"

"Hello, hello, please I need help right away"

I was beginning to panic... I was crying... I was trying to think clearly but it was hard

"My husband is unconscious"... "I don't know how long"

"What... drunk... NO HE IS NOT DRUNK... HE IS DYING!!!"

"Yes he is breathing – barely"

"NO HE IS NOT RESPONSIVE WHEN I CALL HIS NAME!"

"Antonio! Antonio! I'm patting his face but he is not moving!"

"What?"

"I walked in the door and found him on the floor unconscious!"

"I already said I don't know how long …. I just got here!"

"PUT SOMEBODY ELSE ON THE PHONE!

MY HUSBAND IS DYING AND YOU ARE ASKING ME STUPID QUESTIONS!"

Oh God! Please … Please don't let him die too, Please…

That's when I hear the sirens. I ran to the door…

Girl, I have to tell you, I was terrified. I didn't know what happened, how he passed out or why he passed out. Once I actually realized I didn't know how long he had been lying there and that I was cussing him out because he didn't answer the phone while accusing him of sleeping around… and all the time he is dying… I started crying and I had a hard time talking to the operator. I actually had to apologize for yelling at her. She understood that I was hysterical. I'm glad GPS was activated on my phone because emergency dispatch knew where we lived, without me having to tell her. I was almost delirious. He had not mentioned anything about feeling poorly. I have to admit I wasn't paying much attention to him. The medical technicians helped him become a little bit responsive. While they were working with him, I called my family and told them to meet me at the emergency room. I got into the ambulance with him. I refused to leave him and I prayed the entire way because if he died, I would die with him. I keep saying "God please don't make me bury another husband. Please don't." I begged forgiveness for being a terrible wife and if He let Antonio live, I would make it up to him as best I could.

At that moment, I had to admit how selfish I was and that God gave me something good, for me and my children. At that moment I knew I loved and needed him more than I ever imagined I would. I realized God wanted me to be with Antonio and I had performed my responsibilities as a wife disgracefully. If he was having an affair, it was all my fault. I had to figure out a way to get my husband back… if it wasn't too late.

He was slightly coherent and the technician told him he was on his way to the hospital because he collapsed. He seemed relieved to see me, but he looked sort of puzzled or even distressed. He kept saying "I'm sorry, I'm sorry. I didn't want you to have to worry about me." Why would he say that? *"He didn't want me to worry about him?"* He had an idea of why he passed out, but I didn't know anything.

Once in the triage, the doctor came in, shook my hand, then turned to Antonio and started talking to him, in a very familiar way. However, I'm in shock because the doctor is the woman Maria and I saw him meeting at the restaurant a month ago. He's having an affair with the emergency room doctor. "WHAT IN THE WORLD!!!" My brain was spinning in every direction, but I didn't say anything. And to make matters worse, I was about to have an anxiety attack because I realized I recognized some of the terminology she used.

Antonio is diabetic and has high blood pressure. He has taken Metformin for years for diabetes, but he didn't have to take blood pressure medication because it was manageable. Well it was manageable until the last couple episodes with Wade. He started having migraines. The doctor determined his pressure was too high and prescribed blood pressure medication, which he "sometimes" remembered to take.

Antonio was so engrossed in trying to save the business, he 'forgot' his blood pressure medication. He was working out, eating better, so he assumed he was okay. He had gone to visit Wade in jail. Wade was mean and said very hurtful things to him. That particular day he had not eaten or drank enough water. It was about 96 degrees and the index was over 100+. Traffic was terrible. He was upset about Wade, the business, and probably me too. Shortly after he came home he ate a cinnamon roll and drank a glass of ice water and collapsed. How many times had I told him not to come in from the heat and immediately drink ice cold water… about a thousand!

What the doctor said next really sent my brain reeling. She said, "Mr. Martin, you know with your upcoming surgery you can't afford to have unnecessary issues with your health, especially your immune system and blood pressure. The surgery for prostate cancer is routine, but, if you are sick it will have to be postponed, which is not a good thing. You have to take care of yourself, which includes taking ALL of your medications."

It was as if I wasn't really paying attention until I heard that familiar word – CANCER. I knew about the blood pressure and diabetes and despite how I felt, I was working on changing his health habits from bachelor noodles and burgers to healthier eating options. But when she said cancer, it was as if I had a brain fog and didn't understand what she was saying. I kept saying to myself, "what am I hearing? My husband has… cancer… and I didn't even know it. How long has he known about the cancer? How could I not know?"

"I know exactly how I could not know… because I wasn't paying attention. I was paying attention to what I needed, to what Jamie needed. I didn't want to be bothered with Martin family mess with Wade, even though it was constantly oozing into my private space. And who is this doctor!?"

I was going to throw-up. I ran from the room finding a bathroom just in time. I'm saying, "Oh My God! What is happening here God? Have I been such a horrible of a wife that my husband was sick and I didn't know; maybe I didn't care to know? Are You going to take him from me God? Has he been this sick before? Had he been in the emergency room before? Is that how he met the doctor and now she is giving him full service care? Have I really been that self-absorbed that I didn't have time to notice he was sick? My mother was sick and my dad was too busy to notice. Antonio's mother was sick and his dad was too busy to notice. Are we all an example of the sins of the father passed down? Am I not supposed to have a husband? Is my faith being tested again!? First James and now Antonio?"

I was on the floor in the bathroom crying and begging God to let me keep my husband and promising to do better. Just then I had a flashback of Justin bargaining with God for our mom's life. Then someone knocked on the door, so I tried to pull myself together. I'm sure my face was streaked with mascara and tears. I got a paper towel, exiting the restroom, trying not to let anyone see how distraught I was. I'm sure they were accustomed to tears in the emergency room. To tell you the truth I don't even know how long I was in there. I headed back to the room, half expecting the doctor to be holding his hand, stroking his hair, telling him she'll be there for him every step of the way. When I walked back into the room the doctor turned to me, telling me she was admitting him for observation. Antonio collapsed because his sugar spiked very high and the possibility existed that he may have had a mini-stroke. Her biggest concern was his cognitive abilities due to the length of time he was unconscious but he seem to be doing well. She also said that had I not come home when I did, he would have died. She said, "Mrs. Martin you saved your husband's life." I said, "No, God saved his life. He just let me help Him." She gave me a very strange look, turned to Antonio and said the strangest thing. "Why haven't you met with the oncologist nurse to finalize arrangements for your surgery? We discussed all of this the day we met at The Restaurant. Since I will be doing the surgery, I really need you to follow the instructions you were given." "This" waving her finger in the air all around his body "was not part of the plan." With a sternness in her voice she said, "If you want to die, let know so that I can help people that want to live, then do whatever you want to do with what's left of your life." But if you want to live and successfully recover from this you must follow my directions. Am I clear?" He said "yes ma'am."

When the doctor turned to me, she saw how distraught I was, turned back to Antonio and said in the most calm, angry voice I have ever heard, "you have not told her, have you?" He said "no." She turned to me apologized for him, and commenced to tell me actually what was going on. Antonio has prostate cancer. It is in the early stages, so we caught it quickly. He had already had some treatments, which might be part of the reason he collapsed. He requires surgery to remove the cancer and as long as it has not spread, he will be fine after radiation. I asked her if she was the oncologist. She said yes. "When was it detected?" "About a month and a half ago." She asked me if she and I could schedule an appointment to meet with the nutritionist while Antonio was in the hospital to schedule a wellness plan for him. I nodded my head and said okay. She didn't question the puzzled look on my face, which was good, because I'm still trying to figure out how the affair fit into all of this. *"Okay yes, I'm slow!"*

When the doctor finished telling me everything, I was dizzy.

She turned to leave the room and said she would return shortly with the admittance order. Antonio had been diagnosed for almost two months, which means he had been sick long before he was diagnosed. The entire time we were dealing with Wade and the problems he caused MMTrucking, Antonio was sick and he never told me anything. He was at work every day, functioning every day, sick every day, and not saying a word to me. *"Why would he do that?"* I know that I was distant, that I had pushed him away, but I couldn't fathom why he wouldn't tell me he was sick, unless he felt I truly didn't care anything about him. Oh my God! I was beyond furious and terrified.

CHAPTER THIRTY-THREE

"Revelation"

When she left, I stood up, stood by him, held his hand and looked into his eyes, trying to find answers. As I touch his hands I could see he was trembling.

"Why are you trembling, are you cold…? I'll have them bring another blanket."

"No, I'm fine."

"In the ambulance when you realized I was there, you kept saying you were sorry and you didn't mean to cause me any trouble." "Why would you say that… what trouble did you cause me?"

"Why didn't you tell me about the cancer?"

"When I found you I thought you were dead… I was so afraid I had really messed up… that I had lost you… that God had taken you from me."

He had a puzzled look on his face.

"What do you mean messed up … lost me? I was trying to follow your wishes"

"I'm sorry, what… my wishes?"

"You were very clear that after your mother, your husband and your son, you didn't want to have to deal with a situation like this ever again."

"Huh, what are you saying? Are you saying you didn't tell me because you thought I wouldn't take care of you?" "Did you really think I would desert you... because you are sick?"

I almost told him I thought he was having an affair, but I caught myself. I could feel the tears streaming down my face as I heard his words echoing in my head. He remembered that conversation from before we were married and took me seriously. He married me thinking that I wouldn't care for him if he got sick.

He said "when I found out about the cancer, I decided not to tell you because I didn't want you to feel obligated to take care of me." I still couldn't believe what I was hearing. He truly believed I didn't care. It was my fault he believed it. After the honeymoon year was over, I just went back into maintenance mode. I made sure I did things wives do. I took care of the house, cooked food, supported him in the business, even let him think I enjoyed sex with him ... which, of course I did ... oh my goodness ... yes I did. BUT I didn't want him to know that. I was stupid and dumb. I did not want him to know I needed him in my life... that he pulled me out of a dark pit. I didn't want him to know that I was vulnerable to him. Dumb and stupid.

This man loved me, probably back in Puerto Rico, but certainly now. He accepted me in my madness. I repaid him by staying in my madness, treating him like a business partner... not like a husband... not like someone I wanted to spend the rest of my life with. If I said it was too dark, do you know he would pull stars out of the sky and placed them above my head. Would I have done something like that for him? Now I would, but then... wouldn't have even thought about it. I showed him kindness, I attended functions with him, I was his business partner and whatever else I had to do that didn't involve showing real love for him. I even put up with his even crazier first wife.

But, I was so selfish. I never wanted to feel hurt, pain or loneliness ever again and because I'd lost someone I loved with my whole heart, I refused to give Antonio my whole heart. I refused to be vulnerable to him or any other man again. And because of my selfishness, Antonio could have died thinking that I didn't love him. Nothing was further from the truth. No matter how much I acted like I didn't love him, no matter how much I told myself that I didn't love him, the fact of the matter is, I was miserable before 'that Tuesday' and I would still be miserable if he had not ignored my madness and married me anyway.

As he dozed off, I left the room to tell the family what was going on and Antonio was being admitted. His sisters said that their dad was so distracted with MMTrucking and with Wade he didn't know their mother was sick. Now they were so distracted with their lives, MMTrucking and, Wade they did not know Antonio was sick. I sat down and cried. Justin sat next to me to console me and Hussein told them why no one knew, other than him and Justin, and they had just found out a week or so ago. The sisters wanted to yell at them, but I told them no, because Hussein was telling the truth. "I'm sure he told them not to tell you, because you would tell me, and he didn't want me to know. He thinks I don't care if he is sick or not."

"How could he think such a thing" asked Maria. "Is that why he's having an affair!" she asked? "OOPS!" said Maria as she covered her mouth. Everyone said "What are you talking about… what affair?" Before Maria could say anything else, I said, "He is not having an affair. The woman we saw is his doctor… his oncologist. She's here at the hospital tonight... I met her."

Hussein said "okay, I'm really confused. Why would you think he was having an affair?"

Maria told them about the night we saw Antonio at The Restaurant. I told them what the doctor said to Antonio, which explained what we saw. "He's not having an affair... although if he were... it would be my fault."

Just then the doctor came to tell us they were about to move Antonio to his room. She explained to us what happened and what will happen in the next couple of days. I told the others I would stay and they could come in the morning.

CHAPTER THIRTY-FOUR

"Room 729: A Family Reunion"

Antonio slept through the night, except when the nurses woke him to give him medication or to check his vitals or some other reason to wake him. I never understood why they wake you up and then expect you to go back to sleep so that they can wake you up again in four hours.

I could hardly sleep. Every time I closed my eyes, all I saw was him lying on the floor barely breathing. All I could think of was, he thought I would not care if he was sick. How selfish had I been? Every time he moved or made a sound I was standing by his bed making sure he was okay. All I have thought about was myself and my pain. I didn't think about how much I was hurting him. But he never showed he was hurting. He just lived life, did everything he could to make me happy; and I did everything I could to stay miserable.

That night I prayed for forgiveness for my selfishness. I asked God not to take Antonio from me just yet. Give me time to show him I was wrong; that I do need him in my life.

I was lying on the couch next to his bed. Sometime during the night I heard him calling me ... "Lizzie!" "Lizzie"... He and my dad where the only humans allowed to call me Lizzie. Somehow I became entangled in the blankets, almost hitting the floor trying to get up. He had the nerve to chuckle, while I'm thinking he is in pain

153

or something. He chuckled more when I realized that I looked a sight; hair all over my head… make-up everywhere, except on my face… mascara streaks down my face where the tears had fallen. I apologized for looking a fright. He said I was beautiful. I told him he was a liar. We chatted for a moment until I couldn't hold it any longer and began crying again.

Antonio asked "what's wrong… please don't cry… I'm okay… I think." "I didn't eat, I didn't take my medicine, I was furious with Wade and it was hot. When I got home I swallowed a cinnamon bun with two layers of icing and ice water… everything you told me not to do. In other words… I almost killed myself." He paused for a moment and then said, "When I was lying on the floor I heard my phone ring; I knew it was you, but I couldn't press the buttons. I tried to answer it but you know what, Jesus told me you were on the way and everything would be okay." I just looked at him and he said, "Yes… I know you thought I was a borderline heathen, but I'm not. Jesus told me everything would be alright because you would be there soon to take care of me; and I just laid there, waiting for you."

I held his hand and kissed him. I told him how sorry I was that he thought I didn't care about him and I wouldn't take care of him. I asked him to forgive me for being so selfish. He said he loved me, planned to live a long time with me and be buried in the same grave, just like his parents. I smiled and kissed him again. He dozed off again. I sat next to his bed until morning.

Everyone showed up in the morning to see how Antonio was doing and how I was holding up. We were both fine.

Grace, Justin and Jamie walked in. I am so happy Justin found his Grace again. He is a changed man. He has found his love for God again and he is so happy. He decided to listen to me and

Jesus and went to our church one weekend when we were out of town. He saw Ms Kelly, Jamie's teacher, who was, Grace, his "sweetheart" from college. They had been "catching up" for about six months but today they were smiling just a little bit more than normal and for some reason I didn't think it was because Antonio was still alive. "Explain the look you all have on your faces" I said. Justin, with a biggest smile I've seen on him in a long time said "She said YES! *Grace holds up her hand and shows everyone a beautiful engagement ring"* as Jamie exclaimed, *"I'm going to be the Princess Bride!"* Lizanne felt tears on her face when she recognized the ring. It was their mother's.

Hussein and Maria interrupted everyone. "We intended to tell everyone last night, but with Antonio hogging the stage and all we decided to wait." We were all like "wait for what?"

Hussein and Maria both chanted at the same time. "We are pregnant!!!!!"

We were all so excited with two family events. A new limb forming on our family tree and Hussein and Maria's child will be the first baby of the next generation born into our family. They did not want to know the gender of their baby. They wanted to wait for God's surprise. Lizanne smiled.

Antonio looked around the room at his melting pot of a family. "We all came from different worlds, but we all ended up in this room as one family. Our parents raised us to be a strong family withstanding the worst attacks; be it hatred, greedy rival companies, mistrust in God and man and even cancer. With God's help we will continue to bond and build our family. We will be an example for all families that no matter what, God is the glue that holds families together, and through Him families can move mountains."

"Beloved, I wish above all things that thou mayest prosper and be in health, even as they soul prospereth." (3John 2)

CHAPTER THIRTY-FIVE

"The thief comes only to steal and kill and destroy..." (John 10:10)

Once or twice Wade wondered if Antonio would ever come back to see him. The 'voices' would tell him not to worry about the half-and-half, "he won't be a problem for long." Wade didn't understand what that meant and after he had not seen him for a while, he didn't worry about it. Nevertheless, as time went on he began to acknowledge all the wrong he had done, how he had been a disappointment to his father and mistreated his brother. He tried to ignore the 'voices' which was something he had not attempted to do before. Even with the medication, they would not stop talking.

One day Esabelle went to see him. He was happy to see her. He told her that he understood why Antonio hadn't been to see him for a while. He was very belligerent towards Antonio that day. She told him Antonio was very sick, which was why he had not visited him. She told Wade that Antonio had a mini stroke and discovered that he had prostate cancer. Wade started to cry which he has not done… ever… at least not because of Antonio. Esabelle assured him that Antonio would be alright and he would visit him as soon as he was strong enough to travel. At that point Wade understood what the 'voices' meant when they said "he won't be a problem for long". They meant that he was going to die! Wade told her it was his fault Antonio was sick; because he treated him so badly, just like it was his fault their father was sick. Wade said to her, "I tried to be good. I tried to ignore the 'voices' but it was too hard. The 'voices' helped me stay angry so I didn't really try to ignore them and now my brother will die because of me. I can't keep this up its too hard." Again Esabelle assured him everyone was fine and looking forward to him getting better and coming home. They chatted for a little while longer and then she left.

As he sat in the room, staring at the piece of glass he found in the court yard, Wade's mind began to fill with hopeless, crippled, suicidal thoughts. Maybe he was better off dead. He had hurt so many people. Because he was angry all the time, he never had a family of his own. He felt he was right where Satan wanted him to be. He remembered something his father said to him when he was around 25 or so while in the hospital recovering from an overdose. He had overdosed because the 'voices' told him *"Take all of the drugs and enjoy this last high."* He did as they said. His dad told him *"Satan's plan is to steal your joy, kill your spirit and destroy your chances of salvation."*

At the time, Wade didn't want to hear any of that. But today, his father's voice would seep through when the 'voices' were quiet. "Satan's plan is to steal your joy, kill your spirit and destroy your chances of salvation." However, the 'voices' kept telling him to *"end it all and stop the pain. Make everyone pay for the misery they caused you."* He thought it would be better by just ending it all. But even in his anger, even in his stupidity, even when the 'voices' were the loudest, he really did not want his soul to be forever lost. Wade was on the floor trying to get away from the 'voices' in his head but they were getting louder and louder.

In the corner of his cell, on the floor, was a magazine someone had given maybe a week ago. He had thrown it in the corner. On the cover was a picture of Jesus embracing a man as he cried and the caption said, "Jesus paid it all, even for me." The 'voices' were screaming "DON'T LOOK AT IT! DON'T READ IT! PICK UP THE GLASS! USE THE GLASS NOW! RELEASE THE PAIN!" When the 'voices' took a breath, his father's word came through to him again, "Satan's plan is to steal your joy, kill your spirit and destroy your chances of salvation. Satan plans to kill you in your sin. If you die in your sin, your soul will be forever lost." Then the 'voices' came back even louder!

Wade sat up on the floor leaning against the bed with the magazine in one hand and the glass in the other hand. Unaware of how long he sat there staring at the magazine cover, staring at the glass and listening to the 'voices' scream at him, and then hearing his father's voice talk to him. Wade looked up at the ceiling and yelled at God. *"You were never there for me, ever!" "Why should I trust You now?" "Why should I believe in You now?" "Give me one reason." "When I open this magazine the answer better be on the first page I see or it will be all over for You!"*

Wade held the magazine up, flicking the pages with his finger, then dropped it on the floor. On the page in a caption box it said, *"Create in me a clean heart, O God; and renew a right spirit within me."* (Psalms 51:10 KJV)

He leaned against the wall and cried again. Wade opened his mouth to talk and the 'voices' started screaming again. Wade cried, *"O God, make them shut up and go away!"* And instantly, the 'voices' were gone. At first he wasn't sure if they were gone. He sat there in complete silence. Finally, God said, *"They are gone Wade. You are fine now. Everything will be different for you, if you chose to be with me, because I still choose to be with you."*

Tears streamed down his face. The last time he had this

feeling of peace was when he stood next to his father in Puerto Rico at his wedding to Marguerite. He begged God to tell his dad he was sorry for everything. He read the text over and over and asked God to forgive him and help him to have a clean heart and a right spirit.

Wade went to the ministry services every week and gave his life to God. It was as if a load had been lifted from his body. One day in a meeting Wade told the group he gave up his old life and has given himself to God, it was now God's turn to give him something... a family of his own. Then he laughed and said, "He did it for old man Abraham, so why can't he do it for me!"

CHAPTER THIRTY-SIX

"You're not heavy ... you're my brother"

Antonio's surgery was successful and although his recuperation was longer than he wanted it to be, he began functioning more like himself. Lizanne went with him to the veteran's hospital for every appointment, making sure he followed all of the doctor's orders to the letter. She loved him back to life.

One day, he decided it was time to see his big brother; it had been entirely too long. Under protest from Lizanne, Justin took Antonio to visit Wade. Wade was very happy to see him, although he was still surprised. Wade had been very mean to Antonio during the last visit. Antonio had written letters to Wade a couple times. He told him about the cancer and other family events, Justin and Graces' engagement and Maria and Hussein's baby. Wade was happy even though he knew he would miss the wedding and wouldn't see his niece or nephew anytime soon.

Wade asked him about the cancer and they talked about what happened the last time he visited. Antonio told him that was the night he had the stroke. He asked Antonio "why did you come back after the horrible things I said?" Antonio said "You are my big brother and I will always love you and be here for you. Do you remember my favorite verse I use to aggravate you with … 'grace and mercy will follow us forever'?" Wade laughed because Antonio learned it wrong but it fits perfectly. He had a hard time holding back his tears of joy, knowing his brother did not hate him, forgave him and that grace comes in all forms.

He told Antonio about his episode with the glass and the magazine, about hearing their father's voice, about his encounter with the 'voices' and God shutting their mouths permanently. Antonio asked him the name of the magazine. He said he couldn't really remember the name but it was something about a message. Antonio said "I wonder if it's Message Magazine. Lizanne has one on the coffee table."

They talked about their dad, Marguerite and about childhood memories. Wade again asked forgiveness for the things he had done while living in his madness. Wade and Antonio had a wonderful visit and many more after that.

Once Wade was released, he moved into the family home in the room his father had always reserved for him. On the wall was a picture of Marcus, with Wade next to him and Antonio sitting on Wade's shoulders. Wade smiled when he remembered that day. He decided to write down all of his good memories. He started going to church with Antonio, Lizanne and Jamie. Janice Colberts was his bible study partner. She knew who he was and was aware of some of his issues. What she didn't know, he told her. They met every week for six months. During those six months he learned how to love himself and love Jesus.

During those six months he also learned what it felt like to love someone. So for the next six months, he and Janice courted. They had a small family wedding. He never knew happiness until he saw her walk down the aisle towards him. Wade remembered how happy Marcus was when he saw Marguerite walking towards him all those years ago. Now, he understood what his father had tried to teach him all of his life. *"Love conquers all."* He was 61 years old.

"Train up a child in the way he should go; and when he is old, he will not depart from it"

Proverbs 22:6

CHAPTER THIRTY-SEVEN

Meeting #17:

"Forever and Ever"

For our last meeting, Lizanne asked me to meet her at their home. She had something she wanted to show me. It was a beautiful evening and the view sitting on the deck looking out at the ocean was unbelievable.

"I wanted to meet you here for two reasons. I want to introduce you to my family. They will all be here in about 20 minutes for a celebration party. Today is the one year anniversary of Antonio's surgery and this week we received the report that he is totally cancer free. He still has health issues to deal with but we are praising God today!"

But, the real reason I wanted you to come is because I want to show you this. This is a picture of Marcus and Marguerite. They are the reason why this family has survived and I would like to dedicate this book, if you decide to write it, to them.

On the back of the photograph was a printed copy of their favorite Psalms – Psalms 145.

Psalm 145 King James Version (KJV)

1 I will extol thee, my God, O king; and I will bless thy name for ever and ever.

2 Every day will I bless thee; and I will praise thy name for ever and ever.

3 Great is the Lord, and greatly to be praised; and his greatness is unsearchable.

4 One generation shall praise thy works to another, and shall declare thy mighty acts.

5 I will speak of the glorious honour of thy majesty, and of thy wondrous works.

6 And men shall speak of the might of thy terrible acts: and I will declare thy greatness.

7 They shall abundantly utter the memory of thy great goodness, and shall sing of thy righteousness.

8 The Lord is gracious, and full of compassion; slow to anger, and of great mercy.

9 The Lord is good to all: and his tender mercies are over all his works.

10 All thy works shall praise thee, O Lord; and thy saints shall bless thee.

11 They shall speak of the glory of thy kingdom, and talk of thy power;

12 To make known to the sons of men his mighty acts, and the glorious majesty of his kingdom.

13 Thy kingdom is an everlasting kingdom, and thy dominion endureth throughout all generations.

14 The Lord upholdeth all that fall, and raiseth up all those that be bowed down.

15 The eyes of all wait upon thee; and thou givest them their meat in due season.

16 Thou openest thine hand, and satisfiest the desire of every living thing.

17 The Lord is righteous in all his ways, and holy in all his works.

18 The Lord is nigh unto all them that call upon him, to all that call upon him in truth.

19 He will fulfil the desire of them that fear him: he also will hear their cry, and will save them.

20 The Lord preserveth all them that love him: but all the wicked will he destroy.

21 My mouth shall speak the praise of the Lord: and let all flesh bless his holy name for ever and ever.

THE

BEGINNING...

Look for AudreyAnn's Books at
https://transitionlifecoach4u.com/order-books

ABOUT THE AUTHOR

Dr. AudreyAnn Moses is a Certified Christian Life Coach, Mental Wellness Counselor, and Best Selling Author (fiction and non-fiction). She is involved in several community-based programs focusing on personal and  professional development and is an experienced workshop/program facilitator. Dr. Moses has written books and articles, and has conducted workshops on personal growth, self-care, and transition. She writes fiction novels addressing situations found in most families. Her stories focus on physical, mental, emotional, relationship, and spiritual trials. Her award winning books are found on Amazon, Barnes and Noble (NOOK), Goodreads, and other venues where books are sold. For autographed copies contact Dr. Moses at (NeverSayCain't Christian Life Coach & Consultant - Order, Books (transitionlifecoach4u.com). AudreyAnn and husband, Leonard, currently live in Greenwood, SC. They have four adult children, ten grandchildren, and two great-grandson which she feels qualifies her as a life coach and to write stories of Christian family dynamics, love, and devotion to each other and to God. Learn more about her coaching services and purchase her books by browsing her Linktr.ee link: neversaycaint | Instagram, Facebook | Linktree